Matthew's words comforted Hope like nothing else.

That's what friends did, comforted one another. So why did she keep noticing the play of muscles beneath his T-shirt? Why was she feeling an electrical charge from being so close to him?

She wasn't attracted to him. She just couldn't be. She was off balance, that was all. Yes, that had to be it. She was out of her usual environment, like a fish out of water. That had to be why she was feeling this way.

The reason she'd let herself close enough to see Matthew's heart and feel her own response...

Books by Jillian Hart

Love Inspired

Heaven Sent #143

Harlequin Historicals

Last Chance Bride #404
Cooper's Wife #485
Malcolm's Honor #519
Montana Man #538
Night Hawk's Bride #558

JILLIAN HART

It's no surprise to anyone who knows Jillian Hart that she grew up to be an author. When she was nine years old she spent every last penny of her savings on a used typewriter so she could type the stories that were always in her head. Over the years her parents endured the loud and rather constant clatter of the keys, and tolerated her daydreaming about her stories when she was dawdling over chores. Because she loved to read and write, she majored in English at Whitman College, where her roommates also endured her typing and daydreaming. After graduate school she worked in advertising and was lucky enough to fall in love with a man who didn't mind her daydreaming or her typing. Now happily married, she is thankful to spend her days working hard at what she loves most—telling the stories that are in her heart. She lives in Washington State with her husband in a little house surrounded by flowers—and a few weeds because she's always typing or daydreaming and sometimes forgets to pull them.

Heaven Sent
Jillian Hart

Love Inspired™

Published by Steeple Hill Books™

STEEPLE HILL BOOKS

Steeple
Hill™

ISBN 0-373-87150-3

HEAVEN SENT

Copyright © 2001 by Jill Strickler

Visit us at www.steeplehill.com

Printed in U.S.A.

You can make many plans,
but the Lord's purpose will prevail.
—*Proverbs* 19:21

Chapter One

Hope Ashton leaned her forehead against the wet edge of the lifted hood and tried not to give in to a growing sense of defeat. Her brand-new rental Jeep was dead, and she was stranded miles from nowhere in the middle of a mean Montana storm. Strong north winds drove cold spikes of rain through her T-shirt and jeans and she shivered, wet to the skin.

How was she going to get to her grandmother now?

Just get back inside the Jeep and think this through. There was nothing else she could do. Hope took a step in the dark and felt her left foot sink into water. Cold sticky mud seeped through the thin canvas mesh all the way up to her top lace. She jumped back, only to sink up to her right ankle in a different puddle.

Great. Just great. But hadn't her life been one obstacle after another since she'd received the call about her grandmother's fall? It was emotion, that's all. Frantic worry had consumed her as she'd tried to book a flight across the Atlantic.

She'd come too far to lose heart now—Nanna was

only a few miles away. God had granted Hope two good legs. She would simply walk. A little rain and wind wouldn't hurt her.

Lightning cut through the night, so bright it seared her eyes. Thunder pealed with an earsplitting ring. Directly overhead.

Okay, maybe she wouldn't start out just yet. She ached to be near Nanna's side, to comfort her, to see with her own eyes how the dear old woman was doing, but getting struck by lightning wasn't on her to-do list for the night. Hope eased around the side of the Jeep, resigning herself to the cold puddles, and into her vehicle.

Warmth from the heater still lingered, and it drove away some of the chill from her bones. As lightning arced across the black sky and rain pelted like falling rocks against her windshield, she tried the cell phone one more time on the chance it was working. It wasn't.

The electrical storm wouldn't last long, right? She tried to comfort herself with that thought as the wind hit the Jeep broadside and shook it like an angry bull on the rampage. Shadowed by the flashes of lightning, a tall grove of trees rocked like furious giants in the dark.

Okay, she was getting a little scared. She was safe in the Jeep. The Lord would keep her safe. She'd just lived too long in cities and had only spent a year of high school here in Montana, on these high lonely plains.

Round lights flashed through the dark behind her, and she dropped the phone. Rain drummed hard against the windshield so she couldn't see anything more of the approaching vehicle. Twin headlights floated closer on the unlit two-lane road, and she felt a little too alone and vulnerable.

Maybe whoever it was would just keep going, she prayed, but of course, the lights slowed and, through the rain sluicing down her side window, she could see the vehicle ease to a stop on the road beside her. Her heart dropped as his passenger window slid downward, revealing a man's face through the dark sheets of rain.

She eased her window down a crack.

"Got trouble?" he asked. "I'd be happy to give you a lift into town."

"No, thanks. Really, I'm fine."

"Sure about that?" His door opened.

Years of living on her own in big cities had fine-tuned her sense of self-preservation. Habit called out to her to roll up her window and lock her doors. But instinct kept her from it. For some reason she didn't feel in danger.

"Don't be afraid, I don't bite." He hopped out into the road, stopping right there in the only westbound lane. "If you don't mind, let me take a look at your engine first. Maybe I can get you going again."

Relief spilled through her. "Thanks."

Through the slant of the headlights, she could see the lower half of his jeans and the leather boots he wore, comfortable and scuffed. He approached with an easy stride, not a predatory one, but she couldn't see more of him in the darkness, and he disappeared behind the Jeep's raised hood.

Maybe it was something easily fixed. Maybe this man with a voice as warm as melted chocolate was a guardian angel in disguise.

Then his boots sloshed to a stop right beside her.

"Hope Ashton, is that you? I can't believe you'd step foot in this part of Montana again."

And then she recognized something in his voice, something from a life that felt long past. When she was a millionaire's daughter from the city lost in a high school full of modest Montana bred kids. She searched her memory. "Matthew Sheridan?"

"You remember me." His voice caressed the words, as rich and resonant as a hymn. "Good, then maybe you'll stop looking as if you expect me to rob you. You've got a busted fan belt. C'mon, I'll give you a lift."

"I'm not sure—"

"This time of night you'll be lucky to see another car. Lower your pride a notch. Unless you think being seen with me will ruin your reputation."

She winced, remembering with a pang of shame the prideful schoolgirl she'd once been. "My reputation has survived worse than accepting help from an old friend."

"We were never old friends, Hope."

"You're not one to sugarcoat the past, is that it?"

"Something like that." Lightning broke through the dark, flashing bright enough for her to see. He appeared taller, his shoulders had broadened, and his chest and arms looked iron strong.

"That was too close for comfort," he said above the crash of thunder. "Let me grab your bags and we'll get you to your grandmother's."

"I can manage on my own." She hopped out, and wind and rain slammed into her. She wrestled with the back door, but a strong arm brushed hers.

"All three bags?" he asked as if he hadn't heard her, his breath warm against the back of her neck.

She trembled and nodded. Words seemed to stick in her throat. It was the cold weather, that was all. That had to be the reason her heart sputtered in her chest.

"You're shivering. I'll come back for the bags. Let's get you inside the truck where it's good and warm." One strong, warm hand curled around her elbow, seeing her safely through the slick mud at her feet.

His behavior and his kindness surprised her so much, she didn't even argue. "You're a gentleman, Matthew Sheridan. I won't forget it."

He chuckled, warm and deep. "I do what I can. Hop up."

The warm interior of his pickup wrapped around her like a hug. She settled onto the seat, dripping rain all over his interior. The dome light overhead cast just enough of a glow to see the rolled up bag of cookies at her feet.

Matthew reached past her and flicked the fan on high. "There should be a blanket behind your seat. Just sit back and take it easy. I'll be right in."

He shut her door, and the cab light winked off. Rain pummeled the roof overhead, and she saw the faint shadows of tall trees waving angrily in the gusty wind. Lightning blazed, thunder answered. She found the blanket behind the seat, just as Matthew said, and noticed three empty car seats in the back seat of the extended cab.

Funny, how life changed. It seemed everyone she knew was married with children and, while she wished them happiness, she certainly didn't believe that marriage could bring happiness. She felt colder and snuggled into the soft thermal cotton blanket that smelled of fabric softener and chocolate chip cookies.

The driver's door snapped open and the dome light illuminated Matthew's profile. Strong, straight, handsome. He'd grown into a fine-looking man. He stowed her luggage, then joined her in the cab and slammed the door against the bitter storm.

"I'll give Zach at the garage a call first thing in the morning." Matthew didn't look at her as he slid the gearshift into second.

Her teeth clacked in answer, and she snuggled deeper into the blanket. The blast of the truck's heat fanned hot air against her, but she couldn't stop shaking.

"I heard about your grandmother's fall. I bet seeing you will cheer her up some."

"I hope so." Her fingers curled around her purse strap. "I plan to stay as long as she needs me."

"Is that so?" He quirked one brow. "I heard you've never been back to visit her."

"How do you know?" His question set her on edge, as if she didn't love her grandmother. As if all the times she'd flown Nanna out to California for every holiday didn't count. Or the vacation they went on every year.

"You didn't show up for the ten-year reunion. Everybody talked about it."

"They did?" Except for a few close friends she'd made, she hadn't even thought of the small town where she'd spent one year of her teenage life. But it had been a pivotal year for her, emotionally and spiritually. "I got an invitation, but I was—"

"In Venice," he finished with a lopsided grin. "I heard that, too."

"I was working."

"On a new book. I know." He slowed down as a pronghorn antelope leaped across the road.

"Look at that." Hope's chest caught. The fragile animal flew through the air with grace and speed. The light sheened on the antelope's white flanks and tan markings. In a flash, it was gone, leaving only the dark road behind.

"I've seen thousands of them, but it takes my breath away every time." Matthew's grin was genuine, and for a moment it felt as if they'd touched.

As if they were no longer practically strangers and all the differences in their lives and in their experiences had vanished. She saw his loneliness and shadows.

Then she tore her gaze from his. She was being foolish, really. She and Matthew Sheridan had nothing in common—the three car seats in the back were proof of that.

Silence settled between them as he drove, and she welcomed it. The loneliness she'd witnessed in Matthew's eyes troubled her. Maybe because she didn't want to be reminded of the loneliness in her life, a loneliness that had no solution. She didn't want love, she didn't want marriage. She didn't even want to feel her heart flicker once in the presence of a handsome man.

She was surviving just fine on her own. God was in her corner, and that was enough. Even on the loneliest of nights.

"Thanks for the ride, Matthew." Her fingers fumbled for the door handle in the near dark. "I know you had to go out of your way."

"Not too far. And it's always my pleasure to help out one of Manhattan, Montana's most esteemed citizens. Or ex-citizens." His gaze didn't meet hers as he hopped out of the truck.

Maybe he'd felt the same way as she did, that when their gazes had met, she'd seen something far too personal. Her feet hit the muddy ground. "Matthew?"

He didn't look up as he tugged out her carry-on, heavy with her computer and camera equipment, and two suitcases. "Go on ahead, get out of this rain. I'll bring your things."

"That's not right." She eased around to take her baggage, but Matthew's grip remained firm on the leather handles. "You've done enough. I'm more than capable of carrying my own bags."

"I'll let you know when I've had enough." As if insulted, he shouldered past her. "I was raised to look after stranded women in distress."

"I've been taking care of myself for a long time."

"I'm sure you have." Matthew set the bags down on the front porch next to the neatly painted swing and pulled back the squeaky screen door.

She'd forgotten how macho and strong men were in Montana. Plus, she figured she was right. She'd seen loneliness in his eyes, a loneliness they might have in common, and that bothered her.

His wide knuckles rapped on the wood frame. "I'll get a hold of Zach at first light."

"Matthew, you've done more than enough. You haven't seen me since high school and—"

"It's just the way I'm made, Hope. Or should I say Miss Ashton?" He tipped his Stetson and backed down the steps and into the darkness, distant but kind. "Give my best to your grandmother."

She opened her mouth, but the words fumbled on her tongue. She didn't know what to say to make things right between them. He'd gone out of his way to help her, as one good neighbor helps another, and instead of recognizing that, she'd put up the same old defenses.

Some lessons in life were hard to let go of, no matter how much she prayed.

She heard Matthew's truck pull away. Red taillights glowed in the black sheets of rain plummeting from sky to earth. She would have to find a way to make things right, to thank him for helping her when he didn't have to.

The door squeaked open, and a woman in a teal tunic and slacks smiled at her. "You must be Nora's granddaughter. Goodness, she's been talking of nothing else all day. Come in, dear. Heavens, but you're soaked clear through to the skin."

"My Jeep broke down and stranded me."

"No!" The nurse looked stricken. "And on a night like this. Haven't seen a storm as bad as this in some time. Was that Matthew Sheridan's truck I saw driving away?"

"He took pity on me and gave me a ride."

"Matthew's a good man. Shame about his wife, though. Let's get you inside and out of those wet clothes, shall we? My name's Roberta—" She made a move to grab the carry-on bag.

Hope managed to get there first, hauling all three pieces into the living room. The nurse had enough work to do without waiting on Hope, too.

"Dear, you're soaked clear through to the skin," Roberta fussed. "Let me draw a bath for you—"

"Thank you, but no." Only one thing—one person—mattered. "How's Nanna?"

"She's been having trouble sleeping."

"Because she was waiting up for me? I called her after supper and told her not to—"

"Why, she can't wait to see you. You and your brother are the only real family she has left." Roberta bustled into the kitchen, flipping on lights as she went. "As I see it, she's got the right to worry about you traveling all the way from Italy on your own. And besides, it's given her something else to think about besides the pain."

Hope's stomach fluttered. She hated the thought of her sweet Nanna suffering. "Is she awake?"

"I'm sure she is. Go on up. Do you want to take this to her?"

Hope took the prepared tea tray, thanking the nurse who'd gone to the trouble, and headed upstairs. She knew each step and knew which stair creaked. Memories flooded back, filling her heart, warming her from the inside out.

Some memories weren't filled with hurt. Like the year she'd spent with Nanna when her parents were divorcing.

As she climbed into the second story, the smell of dried roses, lavender and honeysuckle tickled her nose, just as it had so many years ago.

"Hope? Is that you?" Nanna's voice trilled like a morning lark, joyful and filled with melody. "Heavens, I've worried about you, child. Do you know what time it is?"

"I told you not to expect me until morning." Hope breezed into the room, unchanged from memory with the lace curtains shimmering like new ivory at the windows, the antiques polished to a shine and the wedding ring quilt draped across the carved, four-poster bed. Just like always.

But the woman beneath the covers was fragile and old, changed from the sprightly grandmother Hope remembered.

Deep affection welled in her heart, and she set the silver tray on the cedar chest at the foot of the bed. "Nanna, it's good to see you."

"Come give me a hug."

Hope bent at the waist, lightly folding her arms around the frail woman. Nanna felt delicate and not tough and robust like she'd been at Christmas, less than four months ago. "You smell like honeysuckle."

"One of my favorites. You should have seen last summer's garden! Goodness, the sachets and things Helen and I made. We were busy bees. Why, we had the entire basement filled from floor to rafter with drying flowers." Nanna's eyes warmed with the happy memory, and she patted the bed beside her. "Dear heart, it's good to see you, but you're thinner."

"Been busy." Hope sat on the edge of the mattress.

"Too busy to eat? You work too much. What is it with young girls these days? You should eat, enjoy life, indulge a little."

"Is that what you do, Nanna?"

"Why, it's one of the secrets to a happy life." Trouble twinkled in dark eyes. "I saw your last book. It's absolutely beautiful. Not everyone has the God given talent to take pictures the way you do."

"I'm glad you like it." Hope watched her grandmother's weathered hands lift the hardcover book from the nightstand. "I worked hard on it."

"Love always shows." Nanna's fingers traced her name on the cover, in gold. "It's good work that you do, using your pictures to remind us all the beauty God gives us in each and every day. But work isn't everything in life, remember that."

"You've told me that about a billion times." Trying to avoid a well-worn subject, Hope pressed a kiss to her grandmother's cheek. "You get your rest. We have all tomorrow to talk."

"And what a fine day it will be because you've come home." Nanna returned the kiss. Her fingers held tight and would not let go. "I've missed my Hope."

"Not half as much as I've missed you." A love so sharp it hurt edged into her heart. Hope didn't move away, not until after Grandmother sipped her chamomile tea, whispered her prayers and closed her eyes. Not until sleep claimed Nanna and she was lost in dreams of happier times.

Hope sat in the dark for a long while and watched Nanna sleep. The lightning returned. Rain beat against the window and drummed on the roof, but they were safe from the storm and never alone.

Chapter Two

Hope Ashton. Matthew couldn't get her out of his mind. Not when he'd gone to sleep and not now that the first pink light of morning was teasing the darkness from the sky.

He hadn't recognized her at first glance. She'd softened, grown taller, changed from girl to woman. But that graceful elegance was still there in the fall of her dark hair, in the rich timbre of her alto voice and in every lithe, careful movement she made.

The phone rang, and he turned from the kitchen sink, nearly tripping over a little boy who wasn't quite as tall as his knee. "Whoa, there, Josh. Look where you're going."

The little boy tilted his head all the way back. "Goin' to Gramma's?"

"Almost." He wove around an identical little boy. "Ian, stop eyeing the cookie jar."

"I still hungry, Daddy."

"Hungry? You ate four whole pancakes." He ruffled the boy's dark hair and intentionally turned him away from the counter as the phone continued to ring.

He dodged another identical little boy and snatched up the receiver.

"Matthew? I got your message." It was Zach from the garage. "Got the belt you asked for right here. What happened? That truck of yours leave you stranded?"

"You wish."

"Hey, I'm thinking of my profits," the only mechanic in town teased.

"Nothing like that. I came across Hope Ashton last night, broke down in the middle of that storm. You remember her, don't you?"

There was a moment of silence, then Zach gasped. "Tall, slender, pretty. Nora's granddaughter. Sure, I remember. Is she back in town? Why don't I run the belt out to the Greenley place—"

"Her Jeep's broken down on the highway south of town."

"Then I'll warm up the tow truck and bring it in."

"You can't miss it. Bright red, brand-new model about four miles out." Matthew felt his stomach tighten, as if he didn't like the idea of Zach giving Hope a hand and he couldn't explain why. Maybe it was his conscience.

Sure, the woman troubled him, stirred up all sorts of emotions. He knew he was out of her league— which wasn't why he wanted to help. It didn't sit right backing away now. He liked to see things to the end.

Matthew heard silence and peeked around the doorway into the kitchen. "Ian, stay away from the counter. Go put on your shoes like your brothers."

The little urchin hesitated, tossed him an innocent

grin, then dashed away to join his brothers at the table. Matthew headed down the center hallway and to the front door, careful to keep an eye and an ear on his sons.

"Hope Ashton, huh?" Zach laughed at that. "It'll be something to see her again. I bet she's still a knockout."

"Yep." She was pretty, all right. Model-good looks but there was a girl-next-door freshness to her. A freshness he didn't remember seeing in the unhappy rich girl he'd gone to school with.

Matthew ended the call, checked on the three boys busily pulling on shoes in the corner of the kitchen and went in search of his work boots. He sat down on the bottom step to tug them on.

Morning was his favorite time as the sun rose, so bold and bright. The world was waking up, the birds' songs brand-new and the breeze as soft as a whisper. Peace filled him for a moment, and then he heard a loud crash coming from directly behind him—the kitchen.

That was his two seconds of peace for the day. He took off at a dead run. Six strides took him into the kitchen where he saw his three sons standing in a half circle.

"Josh did it, Daddy!" Kale pointed. "He climbed up on the chair and dropped the cookies."

"They smashed all over the floor!" Ian looked pleased.

Josh's head was bowed, his hands clasped together as he whispered a prayer.

Matthew saw the shattered cookies and stoneware littered all over the clean floor and the pitcher of grape juice at Ian's feet. The refrigerator door stood open and a chair from the table was butted up against the cabinets. He remembered to count to ten.

"We got real hungry." Ian rubbed at a juice stain on his crisp white T-shirt.

"Real hungry," Kale added.

Josh took one look at the floor and bowed his head again. "The cookie jar's still broken, God."

Since he was short on time, Matthew decided to ignore for now the purple stains splattered on his kitchen floor, nudged the refrigerator door shut and grabbed the broom from the corner. "You boys step back. Careful of those sharp pieces."

"Daddy, it's all Josh's fault." Ian tugged on Matthew's jeans, transferring the grape juice from those little fingers onto the clean denim above Matthew's knee.

"Somehow I doubt Josh did this all by himself." He laid his hand against the flat of Ian's back and eased him away from the broken stoneware shards. "Any owies I should know about?"

"There ain't no blood nowhere," Ian announced.

But there *was* grape juice spattered all over the little boy who'd obviously been the one to try to heft the full pitcher from the refrigerator shelf and failed.

One thing was clear. He couldn't go on like this. He needed a new housekeeper or he'd never get off to work on time. "Into the truck. C'mon. Step around the mess, Ian."

"Sorry, Daddy." The oldest triplet looked angelic as he stopped his sneaker in midair, about to crunch right through the cookies and shattered pottery.

He caught Ian by the shoulder, Kale by the arm and was grateful for Josh who clambered after them, muttering an amen to end his prayer. The mess would wait. The boys would have to change at Mom's.

Lord knew, this was all a balancing act. Every morning wasn't as bad as this, but then he was used to having a housekeeper. With three three-year-olds, it made a big difference having another adult to run interference.

Matthew locked the door and herded the boys toward the black pickup in the gravel drive. He opened the door, and the scent of Hope Ashton's perfume— light and pretty—lingered, a faint reminder that she'd sat beside him on the ride to town. Longing swept through him. Not for Hope, but for a woman gone from his life forever.

It had been over two long years since he'd smelled the pleasing gentleness of a woman's perfume in his truck. Two years had passed since he'd buried Kathy, and he still wasn't over his grief.

And how could he? There would never be another woman who would make his heart brighter, his life better.

Kathy had been his once-in-a-lifetime, a gift of love that a man was lucky to know at all. Something that miraculous didn't happen twice.

It just didn't.

Chest tight, he buckled Josh into the remaining car seat and hopped into the cab.

"I'm so glad I have the committee meeting today," Nanna announced as the new day's sun tossed a cheerful pattern across the quilt. "I'll take any excuse I can to get out of this house."

"I thought you were supposed to be on bed rest. How are we going to get you to town if your doctor's orders are to keep you right here?'' Hope slid open the closet door.

''We could always drive. It's easier than hobbling. I'm still not used to those crutches.''

''Very funny.'' Hope pulled out a blue summer dress. ''This would look nice. Before I take you anywhere, I'm checking with your doctor.''

''You worry too much, and I want the yellow dress. The flirty one.''

''Flirty? You're in your sixties. You shouldn't be flirting.''

''That's what you think.'' Nanna's chuckle was a merry one. ''Howard Renton joined the planning committee last month. Both Sadie and Helen made fools of themselves fighting to sit next to him. But I think I won him with my charm.''

''Wear the yellow but don't flirt. Too much.'' Hope laid the cheerful sundress on the foot of the bed. ''Isn't that what you used to tell me?''

''Hope, you're twenty-nine years old. You're *supposed* to be flirting.''

''I'm supposed to, huh? Is there some unwritten law or something?''

''Go ahead and pretend you don't know what I'm talking about. You're going to let the best years of your life slip away alone without a man to love you.''

''I didn't fly all the way from Rome and drive down from the closest airport through a terrible storm to hear that kind of advice.''

''Well, then what kind do you want to hear?''

''The kind that doesn't have anything to do with getting me married off.'' Hope unzipped the dress and lifted it from the hanger. ''‘God gives to some the gift of marriage, and to others he gives the gift of singleness.' ''

'''And the Lord God said, ''It is not good for the man to be alone. I will make a companion who will help him.''''' Nanna lifted her arms as Hope slipped the dress over her head. ''It's not good for a woman to be alone, either.''

''So, the person who marries does well, and the person who doesn't marry does even better.'' Hope smoothed the dress over her grandmother's back. ''I think I've proven my point.''

''You've proven nothing. Love is one of God's greatest gifts. Don't let your life pass you by without knowing it.'' Nanna's hand brushed hers with warmth. ''Goodness, this dress makes me feel young. Fix my hair for me.''

''Do you want it up or down?''

Nanna squinted into the mirror against the far wall. ''Down.''

Hope reached for the brush and started working. ''Tell me more about this man you and your friends are fighting over.''

''He's moved back to town after being away for what, nearly twenty years. He wanted to be close to what remains of his family. Sad, it is. You didn't hear about the tragedy, did you? Lost his son, daughter-in-law and two of his grandchildren in a small plane crash a few years back. In fact, one of the grandchildren was Matthew Sheridan's wife.''

The brush slipped from her fingers. ''I didn't know.''

''Lucky thing, one of the boys got sick right before the plane took off, so she left the children with Matthew. He was devastated. It shook all of us to the core, I tell you. We lost a lot of friends that day.''

Matthew lost his wife and the mother of his children. Her chest tightened. She remembered how he'd seen her safely home last night. And remembered the loneliness in his eyes. ''It's strange to be here after being gone for so many years. All the people I know are much older now. So much has happened to them.''

''And your classmates grown up and married.'' Nanna's eyes sparkled. ''Everyone except you.''

''Surely not *everyone's* married. There has to be a few people in this town as smart as I am.'' She winked at Nanna's reflection in the big, beveled mirror.

''You mean as *misguided*. I think your old friend Karen McKaslin isn't married yet. Now, don't get your hopes up. Her wedding is scheduled for sometime this fall.''

''A mistake.'' Hope shook her head. ''I'll have to give her a call and see if I can't wisen her up.''

Nanna laughed. ''Tease all you want. You never know when the lovebug will bite.''

''Lovebug?'' Hope reached for a headband on the edge of the nightstand. ''If love is a bug, then all I need is a good can of pesticide.''

''Really, Hope. You're impossible.'' Nanna's hand caught hers, warm and accepting, as always. ''And no, I won't change your mind. I'll let God do that.''

''What's He gonna do? Send a lovebug?''

''You never know. There are a few handsome men in this town looking for the right woman to share their lives with.''

"Oh, there are men, all right, but I don't think marriage is what they're looking for."

"Then you've been living in all the wrong places." Nanna winked, then caught her reflection in the mirror. "Oh, Hope. Why, this is wonderful. I hardly recognize myself."

"You look beautiful, Nanna." Hope brushed her hand gently over a few stray wisps, guiding them into place. "What do you want for breakfast?"

"My day nurse Kirby is taking care of that."

"Well, she has enough to do taking care of you."

"Yes, but the real question is, can you cook?" Nanna looked terribly skeptical. "I know how you live, always traveling—"

"That's because I'm always working."

"If you had a husband and a family, you would have more to do with your time than work." Nanna pressed a kiss to Hope's cheek, one of comfort and love. "Go ahead, make breakfast. I'm a brave woman with good digestion."

"I'm not going to poison you."

"And be careful of the sink handle. It's been leaking something fierce. And that right front stove burner is wobbly. I mean to talk to someone in town about it today."

"Have a little faith, Nanna. I'm all grown up. I think I can figure out a faucet handle and an ancient stove."

"'Pride goes before destruction, and haughtiness before a fall.'"

"Relax." Hope helped Nanna lean back into her pillows, then reached for the quilt to cover her. "I'm not going to burn down the kitchen."

"You almost did once, you know."

"I was seventeen years old." Hope pressed a kiss to Nanna's brow. How fast time passed. And it was passing faster every day. "You get some rest, and I'll be right back with some scrambled eggs."

"Now this I have to see," Nanna mused.

Hope pulled the door closed and hurried downstairs, her heart heavy. Nanna was wrong, she didn't need the pain of marriage. She'd watched her parents up close and personal, and she'd sworn never to live like that. Ever.

Even now, remembering, her stomach tensed and she laid her hand there. The ulcer still bothered her from time to time. Usually whenever she thought about her family.

Yes, singleness was one gift from the Lord she intended to cherish for the rest of her life.

"Matthew, you *have* to take my place on the Founder's Days planning committee. I can't do everything." Matthew's mother herded three little boys into her living room. Building blocks clattered and sounds of glee filled the air. "I don't mind keeping the triplets over the summer, you know that. But these three are a lot to keep up to. You're going to have to do some things for me."

"The committee meetings are during the day, and you know I can't take off work. I've got a roof to put on the McKaslins' hay barn—"

"You can work it out. You're self-employed." Mom pressed a kiss to his cheek. "Tell you what, I'll sweeten the deal. I'll keep the boys past supper every night if you'll take over this one tiny, little obligation for me."

"I'm a carpenter. I don't know the first thing about committees."

"Nonsense, a smart man like you. The meeting is this morning, from ten-thirty to eleven-thirty at Karen's little coffee shop. Oh, those boys are a busy bunch, aren't they?" Mom took off at a run. "Ian, don't climb up the fireplace. No, not even if you're a fireman."

There was a twinkle in her eye. The planning committee, as far as he knew, consisted of the town's oldest citizens.

If Mom wasn't playing matchmaker, she was still up to something. If only he knew what.

Manhattan, Montana crept into sight around the last bend. Hope hadn't seen this place since she was seventeen. Last night, when she'd driven through with Matthew, it had been dark and late, the streets deserted.

In the light of day, she saw that much was different from what she remembered. Businesses had changed hands, new stores had come in, but the character and the small-town feel remained.

It was the closest thing to home she'd known in her entire life.

"It's good to be back, isn't it?" Why did Nanna sound triumphant? "I always knew you belonged here, Hope, and not in your parents' world."

"What does that mean, exactly?" Hope braked as an elderly man jaywalked leisurely across the wide, two-lane street.

"It means you're the kind of person who needs roots, like me. To plant them deep and watch your life grow." Nanna tapped her fingers against the dash. "Turn here. Right there in front of the blue shop."

Hope eased Nanna's old sedan into a parking spot. The hand-painted sign on the row of shops read Field of Beans. "I'm not a tree. I don't have roots."

"You know darn well what I mean, you're being stubborn." Nanna opened her door. "Kirby, dear, bring those crutches. I can handle the steps by myself."

Hope saw the nurse's exasperated look in the rearview. "Don't tell me she's always like this?"

"Usually she's worse." The young nurse hopped out of the car, hurrying to help.

Hope listened to her grandmother issue orders to Kirby as she situated the crutches beneath her arms. Nanna might be injured, but her spirit remained unscathed. Hope stepped out into the fresh spring morning to lend Kirby a hand.

Already the sun was hot, and dust mixed in the air. She smelled freshly ground coffee and baking muffins. "Nanna, is there anything you want from the store?"

"Oh, no, you don't." Nanna wobbled to a stop. "You're coming to the meeting with me. You can do your errands-running later."

"But you have Kirby—"

"Kirby has to go fill some prescriptions for me."

"I have to run over to Zach's garage and rescue my Jeep. Then I have to grocery shop." Hope took hold of her grandmother's fragile elbow. "Don't worry, I'll help Kirby get you inside—"

"Look, there's Matthew Sheridan crossing the street." Nanna took a stronger step. "It looks like he's heading for Karen's coffee place, too. Good. I've been needing to speak with him.''

"What you need to do is concentrate or you're going to fall off those things. Maybe we should get the wheelchair from the trunk—''

"Don't you dare. There's only three stairs, and I'm starting to get the hang of these crutches.'' Nanna hobbled forward, then stopped in the middle of the first board step. "Why, Matthew. The man I've been looking for.''

"Me?'' He strolled to a stop on the sidewalk above, his face shaded by the brim of his Stetson. "Nora Greenley. I can't believe you're up and around.''

"It's hard to keep an old warhorse down,'' Nanna quipped as her fingers caught Hope's sleeve. "Matthew, I have a terrible problem up at the house. Now, I could have called the McKaslin boy, but I hear you're a better carpenter. I need some work done on my kitchen.''

"I'd be happy to come take a look.'' He held out his hand, palm up. It was a strong hand with calluses thick on his sun-browned skin. "Do you need help up these stairs?''

"I can handle the stairs. You talk a minute with my granddaughter and find a time she can show you the kitchen.'' Nanna was suddenly busy crutching up the steps and avoiding Matthew's gaze. "Hope, be a dear and handle this for me.''

"You know I can't say no to you, Nanna.'' But Hope *did* feel suspicion burn in her heart. What was her grandmother up to?

"Kirby will see me in, dear. Just make sure you

come and join me. If I need help, I'd hate to interrupt the meeting. You understand.''

"I understand." Was that a twinkle in the older woman's eye? Nanna knew better than to try to fix her up with poor Matthew Sheridan, didn't she? "Try to behave until I get in there, Nanna.''

"You know me." Her crutches creaked against the board walkway.

"That's what I'm afraid of." Hope's chest felt tight watching the frail lady ease her way over the threshold and into the café, as determined as an Olympic athlete.

Matthew leaned against the wooden rail. "Looks like Nora's keeping you busy.''

"Busy? I'm running like a madwoman. It's not even lunchtime and she's exhausted me." Hope couldn't quite meet his gaze. She remembered what Nanna had said about his wife's death. She remembered the loneliness in his eyes. "I guess she wants some work done on her stove and sink.''

"Well, I don't pretend to be the best in town when it comes to appliances, but I can take a look at that sink." Matthew splayed both hands on the weathered rail. "I'm roofing the McKaslins' barn this week. I can drop by, say, Monday morning, if that's no problem.''

"That will be soon enough, I'm sure. I didn't notice any leak when I washed the dishes this morning. I have this funny feeling there's no real hurry. I think Nanna wanted to try to get the two of us together.''

"I had that feeling, too." He shrugged one shoulder uneasily, looking off down the street. "Did Zach get your Jeep fixed?''

"It's repaired and waiting for me. Thanks again for

helping me out. It would have been a long miserable walk.''

"No problem." He tipped his hat, a polite gesture. "Well, I better get going. Don't want to be late for my first committee meeting."

"*You're* on the planning committee?"

"My mom talked me into it this morning. She extorted me, is more like it." A wry grin touched his mouth as he took a step toward the open door. "She's taking care of my sons, so I'm in a bind and she knows it. It's a shame when you can't trust your own mother."

"Or grandmother." Hope hated that she had to follow him toward the gaping door. A bad feeling settled hard in her stomach, the kind that foretold disaster.

"What does that mean?" he asked. Sunlight brushed him with a golden glow, highlighting the wary slant to his eyes. The wry grin faded from his mouth. "You don't think my mom and your grandmother—"

"I sure hope not, but at this point do we give them the benefit of the doubt?"

"I don't know, my mom's been kind of sneaky lately." Matthew shook his head. "And obviously off her rocker. She knows you're only visiting. Maybe it's coincidence."

"Let's hope so, or my grandmother is in big trouble, and I don't care how fragile she is."

"Somehow, I doubt she's in much danger." Matthew caught the edge of the open door and gestured for Hope to go first.

"You haven't seen my temper." Laughing, she breezed by him.

The wind caught her long curls and brushed the

silken tips against the inside of his wrist. His grip on the door faltered, but she didn't seem to notice that the bell overhead jingled furiously. She smelled like spring, like new sunshine and fresh flowers.

"Isn't it marvelous that Hope has agreed to take my place on the committee?" Nora Greenley's voice rang like a merry bell above the clash of conversation in the homey little café. "Matthew, that means the two of you will be working side by side. Doesn't that sound terrific?"

"Nanna!" Shock paled Hope's face. "But—"

"You know I'm not well, dear, and the doctor wants me to get as much rest as possible."

"Yeah, but—" A fall of black hair cascaded across Hope's face, hiding her profile as she leaned her grandmother's crutches against the wall. Embarrassment stained her creamy complexion. She looked at him helplessly.

"It's all right, Hope. I'm getting used to the manipulative behavior of old women with nothing else to do but interfere in my business." He gave Nora a wink so she'd know he wasn't mad. Well, not too mad.

"Watch who you're calling old, young man." But Nora's eyes were laughing at him, as if she were enjoying this far too much. "Helen is calling the meeting to order. She's about to announce Hope is taking over my position. I can't tell you what a relief it is. Hope, dear, come sit down here between me and Matthew—"

It was too late to escape. Helen's voice rose above the sound of the coffee grinder at the counter. And only two unoccupied chairs remained close by. If he wanted to escape, he would have to excuse himself through half of the crowded café.

Hope shot him an apologetic look as she took one of the two remaining chairs. Her hair, unbound and rich, tumbled across her shoulders, catching the sprinkle of sunlight through the curtained window. Her curls shone like polished ebony.

"Now, if Nora is settled," Helen said as the room silenced. "I'll let her tell about how her wonderful granddaughter, whom we haven't seen in quite a few years, has agreed to take her position on our committee. Nora—"

"I didn't agree to anything," Hope leaned close to whisper. "Just so you know."

"Oh, I know." He did. He knew how his mother thought. Mom figured that enough time had passed since losing Kathy and that he ought to get on with his life. The boys needed more than a housekeeper—they needed a mother to love them. And he needed a wife.

But what she didn't know, what she couldn't accept, was that Kathy had been his whole heart.

Regret tightened in his chest until Nora's words and the sounds of the café faded. His parents' marriage had been based on respect, but not true love. Not like his and Kathy's. Mom couldn't understand.

Pain cut like a newly sharpened knife straight through the center of his chest. Mom didn't realize she was hurting him, but she was. Her matchmaking attempts stirred up old memories and grief.

Applause ripped through the café, tearing into his thoughts. The meeting continued, and the sun flirting with the curtains grew warm on his back. Karen McKaslin arrived with coffee and tea for everyone.

Matthew leaned across the table, stretching for the packets of sugar. Hope scooted the little ceramic holder closer, so it was within his reach. She avoided his gaze and maybe it was because she was a woman, soft and pretty, but it made him feel keenly alone.

He remembered a verse from John, one he'd relied on heavily these last difficult years. ''Here on this earth you will have many trials and sorrows. But take heart, because I have overcome the world.''

Matthew stirred sugar into his tea and clung to those treasured words.

Chapter Three

❧

Hope snapped open the kitchen cupboards. "You embarrassed the poor man."

"I don't know what you're talking about."

"Go ahead, play innocent. But I'm not fooled and neither is Matthew." She slammed the cans of food onto the shelves. "It wasn't fair to volunteer me like that. You could have asked me. I would have been happy to do anything for you. Don't you know that? But this—"

"Don't you see? It's for your own good, Hope." Nanna didn't sound quite as confident. "Time is slipping away from me, and I want to know my beloved granddaughter is happy and cared for."

"I can take care of myself." Hope slammed two more cans onto the wooden shelf. "Besides, I'm perfectly happy."

"Sure, but you could be happier." Nanna sighed. "Don't be mad at me, Hope. With this injury I can't serve on the committee, and your spending time with poor widowed Matthew Sheridan can't hurt."

"It's your intentions that bother me. You know how I feel about marriage. And you know why." Hope kept out a box of crackers and folded up the paper grocery sack. "I'm not going to marry anyone. Ever. I'm never going to go through what my parents did."

"Just because your mom and dad couldn't get along doesn't mean that you can't have a fulfilling marriage."

"That's exactly what it means." Hope grabbed the bright yellow box and set it on the table in front of her grandmother. Her chest ached. Old wounds beat within her heart, and she didn't want to be angry with Nanna. "Stop trying to change my life, okay? I like it just the way it is. And no, I don't want a husband. I don't miss having a family."

"But, Hope—"

"Please, just drop it, Nanna. I can't talk about this anymore. *I'm* the result of a bad marriage, remember?" The memories of her parents always fighting, always hurting each other tore through her. Memories she wanted to forget. The wind teased the chimes outside the open window, and Hope spun away, determined to keep control of her emotions.

The past was gone. There was no sense letting it hurt her now. She watched the light in Nanna's eyes fade and she hated that, but she couldn't back down. Marriage was not—and never would be—for her. No matter what. And if she felt lonely in the evenings cooking for one, well, that was a small price to pay for a life without hurt, blame and endless battles.

"What you haven't seen," Nanna continued above the musical jingle of the chimes, "is that some marriages can be a great blessing. Filled with joy and enduring love.''

''Sure, I've seen the movies. I've read the books. Notice how they're all fiction?'' Hope grabbed the teakettle from the stove and carried it to the sink. ''I don't want to hear any more about this, Nanna. Isn't there a passage somewhere in the Bible about minding your own business?''

''Well, Thessalonians. 'This should be your ambition: to live a quiet life, minding your own business—' '' Nanna broke into a chuckle. ''All right, fine, you've won. I'll stop trying to match you up with handsome, kind, marriageable men even if it *is* for your own good.''

''Finally! You've come to your senses.'' Hope grabbed hold of the cold water faucet.

''I'll have you know there are many young women in this town who would appreciate my efforts.''

''Then maybe you should try matchmaking for *them.*'' Hope gave the faucet a twist and felt the old metal handle give.

A blast of cold water slammed against her right cheekbone and across the front of her neck. She jumped back. Water sluiced down her face and dripped off her chin. Her shirt was wet through and plastered to her skin.

She could only stare at the geyser shooting water everywhere—straight up at the ceiling and sideways in every direction.

When Nanna had asked her to talk to Matthew, there really was a problem with the plumbing. She set the broken cold water handle on the counter and swiped more drops from her eyes.

''Kirby, quick, call Matthew.'' Nanna's voice rang

high with distress above the sounds of the cascading waterfall. "Ever since Ethan Brisbane left town, we don't have a decent plumber. Hope, quick, can you make it stop?"

"I'm trying." Her sneakers slid on the wet surface as she tugged open the cabinet doors. She scrunched down and peered under the sink.

The old pipes groaned. Droplets plinked against her forehead. She knew next to nothing about plumbing, but she did own a small condo. She'd had her share of homeowner disasters. "I don't see any shutoff valves. Nanna, how old are these pipes?"

"Who knows? Seventy years or more?"

"Maybe it's time to replace 'em." There was no way to stop the water, not here at the sink. "There must be a shutoff in the basement. I'll see what I can do."

"Hurry, dear, my knickknacks—"

Hope spun toward the sink. The pretty porcelain figurines on the corner shelves above the sink were taking a direct hit.

She stepped into the force of cold water, wincing as it struck like a thousand icy pinpricks. "Kirby, could you help me out here?"

"Sure thing." The young nurse abandoned the phone and hurried across the growing puddle on the floor to carry the rescued figurines to the table. "Mr. Sheridan wasn't in. I got his pager."

"We're going to need someone right away." Hope curled her fingers around the last wet porcelain child. "And it would be better—" she fixed a warning gaze on her grandmother "—if it *wasn't* Matthew Sheridan."

"Don't worry, Hope." Nanna spoke up. "I'm a

defeated old woman resigned to live without a single great grandchild.''

''Sure. Make me feel guilty.'' Hope handed Kirby the last figurine and stood, dripping wet, in the middle of the kitchen. Water crept in an ever-widening puddle across the ancient flooring. As far as she could tell, puddles and crutches didn't look like they would mix. ''C'mon, Nanna, let's get you to safer ground.''

''I'll take her into the living room,'' Kirby volunteered, the crutches already in hand. ''And I'll try to find someone—anyone—to come right away.''

''Thanks, Kirby.'' Hope caught Nanna's elbow as she wobbled, a little unsteady on her feet. ''I'm going to see what I can do downstairs.''

''Now be careful of those narrow steps,'' Nanna warned.

Hope resisted the urge to remind her grandmother that she was no longer a child. The warmth in her chest doubled knowing someone worried over her— that someone still cared.

The water was still spewing like Old Faithful, so Hope ran for the basement door.

No light greeted her when she hit the switch. She guessed Nanna hadn't been down here in a while. She found a flashlight on a hook by the door and searched the lengths of wrapped pipes visible overhead. They ended by the hot water tank in the back corner, where huge cobwebs warned of even bigger spiders.

''No way am I going in there.'' She shivered, her skin crawling just at the sight of those thick, dust-coated gossamer strands.

Then a dark object slinked across the cement floor toward her sneaker. She screamed in midair, already jumping back. The flashlight slipped from her grip. It hit the ground with a crash and rolled, the light eerily aimed at the ceiling. The shadowy spider skidded to a stop, waiting—like he was preparing to launch an all-out assault on her ankle.

"Chances are it's more scared of you." A rich masculine voice rumbled like low valley thunder through the dark. Then boots clipped on the concrete. "He's looking up at you and thinking, boy, that giant sure looks dangerous. I hope she doesn't attack me."

"Matthew Sheridan." She took another cautious step back, her pulse fast, her limbs shaky. "You scared me to death."

"Didn't hear me come down the stairs, huh? I guess you were too busy screaming at this poor defenseless spider." He strode closer, his presence like a fire in the darkness, radiating heat without light. A heat she felt.

"How did you get here so fast?"

"Kirby left a desperate message so I came over. I was next door at the Joneses'." He flashed her a grin in the eerie mix of shadows and knelt down, unafraid. "If you shoo him off, he'll go hide and leave you alone."

"Sure. I feel so much safer knowing he's in the shadows watching and waiting for the right moment to take a bite." Hope tripped back, away from the narrow hallway, not sure which was affecting her more—the spider or the man. "I was trying to find the shutoff."

"Let me take it from here. After all, I'm the professional." He held up a big wrench and stepped into the light. Lemony rays brushed across his face, accenting the fine cut of his profile and the curve of his lopsided grin. "Tell Nora not to worry. I'm on the job."

"Oh, that's a comfort." Why was she feeling like this? The last thing she wanted was to feel attracted to a man. Especially Matthew Sheridan.

She remembered how he'd looked in the coffee shop with sadness so huge in his eyes. How he'd leaned slightly away from her in his chair, placed right beside hers, so that their shoulders wouldn't brush. As if he wanted to make it clear just how much distance he wanted.

Well, he was in luck. She wanted distance, too. And yet, she felt sorry for him. Sorry because beneath his easy grin lurked a great grief, one so obvious how could Nanna even think he'd want to remarry?

Not knowing what to say, Hope backed away, leaving the flashlight on the floor in case Matthew needed it, finding her way through the dark by touch and by memory.

Matthew listened to her light step against the stairs, tapping away into silence. Hope had looked at him like a deer blinded by headlights. Maybe it was the spider or the way he refused to look at her at the meeting today.

Either way, he knew he had to make things right. Since he couldn't back out of his obligation to the committee, it looked like he'd be seeing Hope a lot during the preparations for the Founder's Days dance. He didn't want any strain or bruised feelings confusing things. As soon as he turned off the water and fixed Nora's sink, he'd pull Hope aside and talk with her.

Unfortunately, the old valve was rusted wide open,

and he had to use every bit of his strength to turn it. The old metal groaned, and he whispered a prayer for the ancient pipes to hold. They did, and the rush of water faded into silence.

Overhead he heard the soft tap of shoes—probably Hope's. He tried not to think about that as he brushed the cobwebs off his shirt and retrieved the fallen flashlight. He hadn't looked at a woman since he'd fallen in love with Kathy, and it bothered him. He didn't know what to make of it as he headed upstairs.

Hope was in the kitchen, guiding a mop across the floor. Sunlight spilled through the back door, highlighting the sheen of her dark hair and the agile grace in her slender arms.

She knelt, wrung water from the mop into a bucket, then straightened. "You came to the rescue. Again."

"That I did. I even survived the spider." He couldn't get over the sight of Hope Ashton handling a mop. He couldn't seem to tear his gaze away.

"You're a braver person than I am." She bent to work, swiping with practice. "Sharing dark cramped spaces with arachnids isn't high on my list."

He knew she was from a wealthy family—she probably had her own housekeeper and cook, a chauffeur and gardener—but here she was in simple blue jeans and a light yellow T-shirt cleaning her grandmother's floor with a steady competence. As if she mopped floors all the time.

Not that Hope's lifestyle was any of his business, he reminded himself and he forced his gaze away. But as he crossed the kitchen with water slick against his work boots, he could hear the stroke of Hope's mop back and forth.

"I'm going to have to replace this entire setup."

He checked under the sink to make sure. "Either that, or chances are this kitchen will end up flooded again."

"Then we'll just have you fix it right." Hope swiped her forearm across her brow. "Kirby took Nanna outside for some fresh air. I think she's more upset than she's letting on."

"She's lived here, what, fifty years? It's hard to see something you love damaged." He eased onto his back and adjusted his pipe wrench, determined to concentrate on his job and not on Hope mopping the floor. "I'm going to take out the sink and all these pipes. Put in proper shutoff valves. She'll even get a new faucet out of the deal. Lucky for you, I have a faucet in the carpenter boxes in the back of my truck—I get these emergencies often enough. It's a nice white European one."

"Oh, boy. I can't remember the last time a handsome man gave me a new faucet."

She was kidding—he knew that. But why did his pulse perk up? Did she really think he was handsome? He couldn't see it—he doubted anyone else did, either. That was the thing that made him wary about women like Hope—easy flattery, a drop of kindness, it was superficial and not always innocent. He ought to remember that the next time he couldn't stop looking at her.

Disgusted with himself, he gave his wrench a hard twist, and the old pipe came loose from the wall. "So, you'll be staying in town through Founder's Days?"

"If Nanna needs me that long." Hope knelt to wring the mop. Water splashed into the bucket. "I'm sorry about the committee meeting. She's just trying to throw us together. I hope you know I had nothing to do with that."

"I figured it out easy enough." He slid out from beneath the sink and caught sight of Hope hefting the full bucket toward the back door, so at odds with what he expected from her. Maybe that's why his gaze kept finding her in the room. "I believe you. Remember, my mom blackmailed me."

"Your own mother? That's hard to believe. I remember how sweet she was." Hope disappeared in the shimmer of the midday sun.

"Sweet? Sure, she once was, I suppose. Then she became a grandmother and started meddling."

Hope breezed back inside, swinging the empty bucket, and her smile looked genuine enough to make his heart flip. She lifted one delicate brow. "Meddling?"

"Yep. Mom decided she wanted more grandchildren so I needed another wife to provide her with some." He concentrated on coaxing the broken faucet out from the tiled wall. "It's a desperate situation."

"I understand that completely. Poor Nanna won't be happy until she thinks I'm taken care of." The mop smacked against the floor. "She isn't satisfied when I say I can take care of myself. As if any man will do."

Any man. A common, middle-class working man. Matthew knew it wasn't a fair way to think, but even though Hope Ashton looked kind and casual and good-hearted and even though she was mopping a floor, she was a millionaire's daughter. She was a renowned photographer. She wasn't looking for just any man.

The pipe stuck, and he gave it a hard tug. It split into pieces and tumbled into the sink. "These pipes look as old as the house."

"I'm sure they are." Hope swept past him, leaving a lingering trail of sweet, light perfume. "Grandfather was notoriously frugal. Do you think you can get the water at least running today?"

"Sure can." He shook his head at the rot where the pipes had been leaking for some time. Better to concentrate on his work. "This wall is going to have to be replaced. And this set of cupboards."

"Nanna is going to be heartbroken. Grandfather made those cabinets for her. They're custom—"

"I'm not a bad carpenter. I bet I can match them." He couldn't help teasing her, she looked so serious, so concerned. "Have a little faith, Hope."

"I'm trying." She smiled, soft and sweet, and he noticed the way her dark curls caught the light, shimmering like rare silk.

Heaven help him.

A bell rang, spinning her toward the front door. Long locks flicked over her shoulder, glimmering with such beauty he couldn't look away. She hustled from his sight, padding across the damp floor and into the dim recesses of the entry hall.

He recognized Helen's voice and then heard only silence. Hope must have taken her out to see Nora in the flower garden. Matthew headed out the back door to grab what he needed from his truck. He'd put in new pipe, valves and a faucet.

An older lady with a broken leg needed running water. He figured the McKaslin family wouldn't mind if he was a day late finishing their barn.

* * *

"How are you and Matthew getting along?"
Nanna asked after she'd greeted, Helen, her lifetime
friend. "Did you notice how wide his shoulders are?
I just love a man with broad shoulders."

"Then *you* flirt with him," Hope teased as she
tucked a cushion in the black metal chair for Helen.
"Let me fetch some iced tea. I'll be right back."

"She's hurrying back to him." Nanna's loud whisper carried on the sweet breezes.

"To look at his shoulders," Helen teased.

Okay, so his shoulders *were* broad. Hope hopped
up the back steps and she couldn't help it—her gaze
found and traced the strong line of Matthew's muscled arms, corded as he worked to set the new pipe
in the wall.

"Would you like some iced tea?" She reached into
the cupboards for three glasses, determined not to notice his well-honed physique.

"Sounds good." He didn't look up from his work.
As if he were afraid to make eye contact with her.

Why now? Then she noticed the windows were
open, and Nanna's voice lifted on the breeze through
the window. He couldn't have accidentally overheard
what they were talking about, right?

The curtains fluttered with a gust of wind. "Goodness, Hope is so alone. Matthew's mom and I thought
since they were both so lonely, we'd try to toss them
together—"

The curtain snapped closed, cutting off the rest of
Nanna's words.

A cold feeling gripped Hope's stomach. She felt
her heart stop as she met Matthew's gaze.

"I guess that's as close to a confession as we're

going to get." He stretched a kink in his neck, flexing the muscles in his left shoulder and arm. "Our own families are working against us."

"Nanna just promised to stop—" Hope's knees felt weak. "No, she didn't exactly say that. She sort of skirted the issue and changed the subject. You heard her. She doesn't sound one bit sorry."

"It sure didn't sound that way."

Hope set the pitcher on the counter. She remembered how he'd looked in the coffee shop, lost and sad and brokenhearted. "I'm sorry, Matthew. This must be painful for you."

"I'm used to it." His words were as warm as spring rain. "*This* is what I've been up against ever since the boys wanted a mother for their third birthday. My mom has been on a nonstop campaign to find me a wife, and now she's involving her friends in the search."

"Like any woman will do, right?" It hurt to see the shadows in his eyes, so deep hazel and mingled with pain. She didn't know what to say. How to comfort him.

He laid a packaged faucet, shiny knobs wrapped in plastic, on the counter. "It sounds to me like these women are pretty determined. Just how do you think we can stop them?"

"It's going to be a long awkward summer unless we find a way."

Matthew rubbed the heel of his hand against his brow. He looked tired. He looked as if a world of burden rested on those wide shoulders. Her heart ached for him.

She poured iced tea into the three tumblers, and then inspiration gripped her. "I know! Proverbs. 'If you set a trap for others, you will get caught in it yourself.' ''

"You mean..."

"Have you noticed how your mother and my grandmother have all this time on their hands? Notice how they both live alone."

"I noticed." Light began to twinkle in Matthew's eyes.

"Poor lonely widows. With no one to take care of them." Hope tugged the curtain aside and caught sight of Nanna in the garden shaded by the tall maple. "Nanna mentioned a certain older gentleman she thought was very attractive. Maybe there's someone your mother might like...."

"Hope, you're a genius." Matthew laughed, relief chasing away the shadows in his eyes and the furrows from his brow. "We turn the tables on them. And why not?"

"That's right. Why not?" She topped off the last tumbler and handed it to Matthew. "Your mother and my grandmother had no qualms about torturing us."

"That's right. We find the two of them husbands, and they'll be so happy they'll forget all about us." Matthew leaned against the counter and sipped his tea. "It's not deceptive. After all, we're bid to let love be our highest goal...."

"Like Nanna said, it's not good to be alone." Hope felt the sunlight on her face, warm and sustaining. She knew Nanna wasn't alone, not truly, but she also remembered how years had slipped from Nanna's face at the thought of Matthew's handsome grandfather-in-law.

Nanna had spent too many years in this empty house watching for the mailman to slip letters into her box or waiting for the phone to ring. That was about to change. Hope could feel it down deep in her soul.

Maybe that's why the Lord had brought Matthew to her in the middle of that dangerous storm. And why Matthew stood here now.

If God kept watch over the smallest sparrow, then surely He cared about the loneliness in an old woman's heart.

Chapter Four

The new morning's sun had already burned the dew off the ground as Hope made her way through the neighbor's fields. Dark green, knee-high alfalfa swayed in the warm breezes and brushed her knees as she spotted the Joneses' barn and the man kneeling on its steep peak, tacking down new gray shingles with a nail gun.

She only had to look at him for her heart to flip in her chest. For one brief moment she noticed the wind tangling his collar-length hair and let her gaze wander over the lean hard height of him. In a white T-shirt and wash-worn jeans, he was a good-looking man. As if he felt her gaze, he glanced up from his work and shaded his eyes with one gloved hand. Then he waved in welcome.

A prairie dog gave a chirp of alarm and scampered out of sight as Hope hurried through the field, alfalfa shoots brushing against her bare skin. Matthew disappeared from the roof only to reappear circling from behind the weathered barn, stripping off his work gloves.

"Hey, I began to think you stood me up."

"I know, and I'm sorry. Nanna was in a lot of pain this morning and we couldn't get her to eat. I finally tempted her with fresh cinnamon rolls, but it took more time than I figured." She held up a paper sack. "I brought a peace offering, though. Figured you couldn't be too mad with me if I brought sweets."

"A wise woman."

"No, a grateful one. You've helped me twice now, and I'm indebted. The cinnamon rolls are only a start."

"You don't owe me a thing." Matthew flicked his gaze away toward the west side of the barn where shade stretched over soft grasses in an empty corral. "I've got a cooler with juice over here. Let's get down to business."

"Sure." She followed him past the wooden posts, worn gray from time and the elements, and when she saw the blanket spread out on the small patch of wild grasses, she realized that Matthew had gone to some trouble. She regretted being late.

"Tell me how the new kitchen plumbing is working out," he said over his shoulder as he knelt down in front of a battered blue cooler.

"Nanna's happy with your work, but she's fretting over the ruined cabinet."

"It shouldn't be long until I have the replacement for her. I planned on tooling it in my workshop at home this weekend. Tell her I won't forget to come by and make the cabinet as good as new."

"Oh, I think she can't wait to get us in the same house together." Drawing closer, Hope knelt on one edge of the fleece blanket. "After you left last night, she kept going on and on about all your wonderful attributes."

"She had to resort to lying, huh?" His eyes twinkled with merriment.

And she felt that twinkle in her heart. "I can see a few good things about you, Matthew, not that either of us is interested in the way Nanna thinks. I tried to tell her that you were more interested in fixing her ancient pipes than in making small talk with me, but she wanted to know every single word we exchanged when we were alone in her kitchen."

"She couldn't hear us well enough from the garden, huh?"

"That's what I thought, too." Hope unfolded the neat crease at the top of her sack, and the fresh scent of frosting and cinnamon made her stomach rumble.

Matthew handed her an unopened juice box and knelt down a fair distance from her. "My mom was singing your praises last night when I went to pick up my boys. She had that same look in her eyes that Nora had."

"You're right, they are shameless meddlers and they need to be taught a lesson." She held out the bag to him.

He reached inside and withdrew a gooey pastry. "Now I'm doubly grateful you came by. These cinnamon rolls are the best things I've seen in a long time. Nora's baking is famous county-wide."

"Nora's recipe, but I baked them."

"*You?*" Did he have to look so surprised?

"Hey, I have my uses. I packed enough for you to take home to your boys." She took one sticky roll and plopped the bag on the blanket between them.

"Now, wipe that shocked look off your face and tell me. Do you have any idea who your mom might be interested in?"

"Not one. I'll have to pry into her life a little, like she's been doing to mine lately." He sank his teeth into the roll and moaned. "I took a long hard look at Mom last night, and I figure she's got to be lonely. I've got my boys, but when the day is done, she's alone."

"Nanna's the same way. It's got to be sad. All the work they did and the sacrifices they made to raise their families, and now, when they should be enjoying their lives, they have no one to share with."

"Do you know how we can fix that?"

"Not really. I was hoping you'd have a brilliant idea and get me off the hook."

"Give me another cinnamon roll and we'll see what I can come up with."

He's deeply lonely, too. Again, Hope felt it with the same certainty as the gentle breezes on her face. She wondered if he sat up at night, watching the late shows or reading to the end of a book just to keep from going to bed alone, as she did. She wondered if he, too, had a hard time sleeping with the dark and the silence of the night, when prayer could only ease the empty space....

"Nanna let it slip that she has a crush on Harold."

"Kathy's grand dad?" Matthew nodded slowly as he helped himself to another roll. "I noticed Helen fought to sit next to him at the Founder's Days committee meeting, but I didn't know Nora was interested in him, too."

"He wouldn't be lonely, would he?"

"He's been a widower as long as I have." Matthew

stared down at the pastry and didn't take a bite, the sadness in his eyes stark and unmistakable.

Maybe Nanna was right, Hope considered. Maybe, every now and then, true love was possible. Every now and then.

"I'm taking the boys to see him at his ranch this weekend. Between chasing after my sons, I'll try to figure out if Harold is interested in Nora."

"And if he is, we could casually set them up so they wouldn't know it was us. Something not as obvious as what they did to us on the Founder's Days committee."

"Sounds like a good plan." Matthew took a bite of the roll, but the sadness remained in his eyes. The breeze tangled his hair, tossing a dark hank over his brow, and she fought the urge to brush it away, fought the urge to reach out and try to comfort him.

"How's the roof coming along?" she asked, not knowing what else to say to change the direction of their conversation. She stood, drawn toward the ladder stretching twenty feet in the air, and studied the roof's steeply pitched slope. "Do you mind if I climb up?"

"Yeah, I mind." He leaped to his feet, all business, square jaw set and hands fisted. "You could fall, and then what would I say to your grandmother?"

"I won't fall." She spun around, taking in the expanse of the river valley bright with the colors of spring, and ached for her camera. "Okay, I'm not interested in your roofing job, but on the walk over here my mind clicked back to work and I could get a great view from up there."

"You can get a great view of the valley from the road."

"Yeah, but I'm already here." She grabbed hold of the ladder and fit her sneaker onto the weathered rung.

"Hope, I'm not kidding. You're going to break your neck." But he didn't sound too upset with her.

When she looked over her shoulder, she saw that he was holding the ladder steady for her and shaking his head as if to say women didn't belong on ladders. Well, she wouldn't be on for long. "I appreciate this, Matthew."

"If you weren't helping me out with my mom, I'd let go of this ladder."

"Sure you would. You're too nice of a guy."

"That's only according to rumor. You can't trust everything you hear."

"Nanna says a man who can raise three small boys at the same time has to have the patience of Job and the temperament of an angel."

"Either that or he's on psychiatric medication."

Hope stumbled onto the roof, laughing, but Matthew hadn't fooled her. Sure, he was joking, but there was no way he could disguise the patience and good humor lighting him up from within, not quite chasing away his sadness. It touched her somewhere deep inside her well-defended heart. How was it that *this* man could affect her so much and so quickly?

"Be careful up there." The ladder rubbed against the weathered eaves with each step Matthew took as he climbed higher. "I don't want to have to explain to Nora how I let her only granddaughter tumble off a barn roof. I'd never get work from her again."

"Repeat business is all that matters, is it?"

"Sure." He hopped onto the roof with an athletic prowess that drew Hope's gaze, and a slow smile tugged at the left corner of his mouth. "Now before you start running around up here, some of the shingles aren't tacked down yet."

"I noticed that. Really." Wisps had escaped from her ponytail, and she swept them back with one hand. "Between you and Nanna, I feel like an awkward kid again. Stop worrying about me, okay? I'm not going to take a nosedive off the barn. I've been on a roof before."

"Not as often as I have, I bet." He curved his hand around her elbow, holding her secure. "Just in case."

"I'm not afraid of heights."

"I am."

"You? Manhattan's best carpenter?"

"My roof jobs would dry up if word like that got around. You'll keep my secret, right?" His grip on her arm remained, sure and steady, keeping her safe.

"I don't know," she teased in turn, heading toward the roof's peak. "Seems to me keeping a secret like that could be worth some money."

He chuckled, rich and deep, and it somehow moved through her even though they hardly touched. Like a vibration of warmth and sunlight, she felt it, and when her sneaker hit a loose shingle, his grip on her arm held her steady even before she could stumble.

His touch remained, branding her with his skin's heat, and she almost stumbled again. Why was her heart beating as if she'd run a mile? With every step she took, she was aware of the way he moved beside her—the easy, athletic movements as he escorted her safely to the peak of the sloped roof.

No, she *wasn't* attracted to him. He was simply being a gentleman, as he'd been when he'd carried her luggage and driven her home on the night of the storm. A gentleman, nothing more and nothing less, and even if that was attractive to her, she didn't need to panic. He was no threat to her heart. No threat at all.

She faced the wind, and the sweet country breezes lifted the hair from her brow and whirred in her ears. Sunlight slanted in ragged, luminous fingers from the wide blue sky to the rich green earth.

"I should have brought my camera. Look at the cloud shadow on those hills."

"The Tobacco Roots." He nodded toward the wrinkled hills in the distance, rugged and rocky, in contrast to the regal Rockies to the West. "Kathy and I used to hike there before the boys were born. We tried it once afterward, carting the three of them in backpacks, but they were hot and miserable and, unfortunately, teething. We decided not to make that mistake again."

"Scared away the wildlife, did they?"

"I still think half the deer never did return to their natural habitat. The park ranger threatened to ticket us." He shrugged one capable shoulder but his grin didn't reach all the way to his eyes.

"I remember Kathy. She was two years behind us in school, wasn't she?"

"Yes." A muscle worked in his jaw as he towered over her, his back to the sun, his face shadowed.

Hope sat on the hot shingles, emotions tangled into a knot in her stomach. She didn't want to say anything more that would make sadness shade his eyes. "How old are your boys?"

"Three, almost four. Their birthday is in July."

"Triplets. That must be a handful."

"When Kathy was alive, it was *almost* manageable. When we finally got them on the same sleeping schedule, that is.'' The sadness crept into his eyes anyway as he sat down beside her, leaving a deliberate space between them. ''Right now I'm between housekeepers. It's hard to find someone with the right temperament.''

''I bet it isn't easy keeping up with triplets.''

''It's not impossible. They are something, I'll tell you that, always going in different directions at once, but I wouldn't trade 'em for the world.''

The wind tossed dark shocks of hair over his brow as he looked everywhere but at her. ''I haven't seen the world like you have, heck, I haven't even been out of Montana, but I have everything I want right now. I have my boys and that's all I need.''

''Then you're a lucky man.''

''I'm not going to argue with you about that.''

His voice dipped and he turned away from her to study the valley spread out before them. As the silence lengthened, Hope tried to pretend she wasn't touched by what she'd seen in Matthew's eyes and heard unspoken in his words, but she failed. She *was* touched. Anyone could see a father's steadfast love in him as certain as the warm sun overhead.

Not that what lived in Matthew's heart was any of her business.

Maybe this jumpy, skittery feeling wasn't an attraction to Matthew at all. Maybe she was itching to start working again. That's it. ''I'd better get back before Nanna misses me.''

Matthew stood, not meeting her gaze, and offered his hand.

She straightened on her own, not certain if she could touch him one more time. She *wasn't* attracted to him…and she didn't want her physical reaction to him proving her wrong.

"Looks like we're in trouble." Without looking at her, he nodded across the field toward the dirt road, where a dust plume rose behind a sedate burgundy sedan. "It's my mom. No, there's no time to run. There she is. We're busted."

The look of dismay on Hope's face told Matthew she didn't like the prospect of being caught alone with him, and he couldn't blame her. Mom would jump to conclusions and only take seeing them together as encouragement. He held the ladder for Hope so she could climb down safely.

She knelt and carefully placed her designer sneakers on the top rung. "Sure, send me down first into enemy territory."

"Better you than me. Mom will show you mercy."

"Not if she's anything like Nanna."

Her attempt at humor touched him because she couldn't like this situation. It was absurd that anyone would think that a small-town carpenter belonged anywhere near a millionaire's daughter.

"Daddy! Daddy! Daddy!" The words rang on the air the instant the passenger door of Mom's car swung open. As Hope finished descending, Matthew watched his sons race full out toward the fence until Mom shouted at them to wait and not touch the barbed wire.

Hope lighted on the ground and tilted her head back to look at him. "I didn't know they were identical."

"Keeps things interesting."

"I bet it does." She covered her eyes with her free hand and squinted through the glaring sun to watch the triplets tumble into the field.

He started down the ladder, descending quickly. Already Mom was helping the boys through the fence and there was no mistaking the look of delight in that grin of hers, which he could see plainly from across the field. This wasn't what he needed. Mom would think she was on the right track and start really pushing.

"Daddy, Daddy, Daddy!" The triplets plowed through the sweet-smelling alfalfa and scrambled to him, arms flung open.

Matthew barely had time to brace himself before the boys threw their arms around his knees and held on tight, bouncing and shouting. "Did you three give your gramma so much trouble she decided to give you back?"

"It was tempting," Mom teased over the racket of the boys talking at once. He heard the words "fire," "fireman" and "big truck." "Agnes had a small kitchen fire and wanted you to give her an estimate on the damage."

"You could have called, Mom." Matthew lifted Josh onto his hip.

"Yes, but you know I hate talking to that beeper thing of yours. Hope, what a pleasure to see you again." Mom practically beamed as she approached the slim woman who stood off by herself, as if not sure what to think of them all. "I heard from Nora you were in town."

"She finally figured out a way to get me back here." Hope took Mom's hand, her manner warm, as if she wasn't upset in the slightest. "It's good to see you again, Patsy."

The boys demanded Matthew's attention, telling him everything about the sirens and the big red truck, but his gaze kept straying to the woman talking with his mother, whose girl-next-door freshness was at odds with everything he remembered about Hope Ashton from high school.

"Is that lady gonna take us?" Josh asked, both fists tight in Matthew's T-shirt.

The other boys turned to frown at Hope, and before Matthew could answer, she did.

"No, but I did bring you boys something." Hope swirled away from his mother and snatched the paper bag from the blanket.

Of course, his mother took one look at the blanket, not an item he usually took to work with him, and lifted one curious—or was that accusing?—eyebrow.

Ian took one step forward, interested in Hope's paper bag. "Cookies?"

"Candy?" Kale looked tempted.

Josh buried his face in Matthew's shoulder and held on tight.

Matthew watched as Hope shook her head, dark wisps tangling in the wind, and knelt down, opening the sack. "If you boys don't like cinnamon rolls, I could eat them all by myself—"

"Cinnamon rolls?" Kale shot forward, not caring if this woman was a stranger. "Like the kind Gramma makes? With frosting?"

"With frosting."

Ian scrambled closer. "Does it got raisins? Don't like raisins."

"No raisins, but they do have icing. Go ahead and try one." Hope shook the bag, as if she were trying to coax them closer.

Huge mistake. Matthew set out to rescue her as both boys plunged their hands into the sack, fighting for the biggest roll. But Hope only laughed, a warm gentle sound that made him stop and really look at her, at this outsider who had never quite belonged in their small Montana town.

She didn't look like an outsider now. Her faded denims hugged her slender legs with an easy casualness, and her T-shirt was probably a big-label brand, but the cherry-red color brought out the bronzed hue of her skin and the gleam of laughter in her eyes. She didn't look like a millionaire's daughter and an established photographer.

She looked like a beautiful woman who liked children. His children.

"No, only take one." She merely shrugged when Kale got away with two plump rolls, and Matthew was about to make Kale put the pastry back when Hope shook her head, her cheeks pink with laughter, her eyes bright and merry. "Good thing I brought enough for second helpings."

Josh buried his face harder into Matthew's shoulder and held on tighter.

"He's sensitive." Matthew leaned his cheek against the top of the boy's head. "We've gone through a lot of baby-sitters and it's been hard on him."

"I know exactly what that feels like. I had a lot of different nannies when I was little. All that change can be hard." She pressed the bag into Matthew's free hand. "He might be interested once I'm gone."

Why did he feel disappointed that she was leaving? "So, you're leaving me alone with my mom?"

Hope glanced over her shoulder to watch his mother sit Ian and Kale down on the blanket, admonishing them to eat with their mouths closed. "I bet a grown man like you can handle anything and besides, I don't want to be in the way."

"You're welcome to stay." And it surprised him because he meant it.

"This will be the perfect opportunity to talk with your mother and try to figure out who we should fix her up with." She backed away, lifting a hand to wave at Mom and the boys.

"I hope to see you again soon," Mom called. "Say thank-you, Ian, Kale."

Two thank-yous chimed in unison.

Matthew watched helplessly as she breezed away from him, the big blue sky at her back, the green field at her feet. He wanted to stop her, to keep her here with him. It didn't make a bit of sense, but that's how he felt. He couldn't help it.

He watched as she turned around to glance at his boys eating unfurled sections of their cinnamon rolls, sticky and happy, and the look in her eyes, the softness on her face made his knees weak. He had to lean against the corner of the old barn for support.

Was that longing he saw on Hope Ashton's face? Before he could be sure, it was gone. She shouted across the widening distance. "I'll tell Nanna you haven't forgotten about repairing her cabinets."

"Sure." He felt tongue-tied, not sure what to say as she spun around and headed off through the fields, leaving him with a strange, yearning feeling.

A feeling he decided he wouldn't look at too closely.

"Those boys are the cutest things I ever did see," Nanna crooned as Matthew's triplets tripped down the church aisle, their father towering over them. "And

Matthew is cute in an entirely different way. Why, if I were you, Hope, I'd cut a path for that man, I tell you. He's as dependable as the day is long, and you already know he'll make a wonderful father. Look how he handles those boys.''

"I'm immune to the lovebug, Nanna. Don't get your hopes up because I'm not planning on marrying anyone.''

"Still, Matthew is a very handsome man.''

"He's still grieving his wife, Nanna. Have you and Patsy given one thought about how much your match-making is hurting him?''

"Well, if that's true, then I'm sorry about that, but honestly, grief does fade, maybe not completely, but there comes a time when you're ready to start accepting what life has to give.'' Nanna's hand covered Hope's and squeezed gently, lovingly. "In time a heart is ready to love again.''

"You've been a widow for over ten years.''

"That I have.'' Her sigh was sad, and the old lady looked hard at the stained glass windows bursting with color beneath the sun's touch. "But I'm more concerned about you. You should be thinking about starting a family of your own. Patsy told me you went to see Matthew for a little picnic the other day.''

"No, I went to remind him about your cabinets.''

"With cinnamon rolls?''

Hope glanced around, desperate for a change of subject. She spotted an elderly man, his back straight and his shoulders strong as if he'd done battle with age and won, his gray hair distinguished as he strode powerfully down the aisle toward Matthew and the triplets. "Look, there's Harold. I can see why you have a crush on him.''

"It's probably foolish, but I—" Nanna stopped, the brightness in her eyes fading. "I'm just having a little fun, and it makes me feel young again."

Hope wondered at the change in her grandmother, and when she saw Helen hurrying down the aisle to speak with Harold, she knew why. Helen might not have any idea how Nanna felt about the handsome older gentleman, and Hope knew that Nanna wasn't about to say anything differently now.

Organ music broke through the din of the congregation settling onto the old wooden pews, and disappointment wrapped around Hope's heart as Helen took Harold by the arm and led him to Matthew's pew.

"It's not like I'm crazy over the man or anything," Nanna said staunchly, but her voice sounded too tight and strained to be telling the truth. "But a handsome man is always a joy to behold."

Six rows ahead of them, Matthew stood to greet his grandfather-in-law. Patsy was there and ordered the boys to squeeze closer together to make room, and there was enough space on the bench for Helen to settle down beside Harold.

As if he felt her gaze, Matthew turned and found her in the crowd. He wore a dark suit and a white shirt that emphasized his sun-browned, wholesome good looks, the kind a man had when he worked outside for a living.

Her heart gave a strange little flip-flop.

"I'm sorry," he seemed to say as he shrugged.

She shrugged back. Matchmaking wasn't as easy as it looked.

Sad for Nanna, Hope wrapped her arm around the old woman's shoulders and held her tight. They were

in God's house. Surely here of all places He could
gaze into the old woman's heart and see the loneliness—and now the hurt.

Please help her feel young again, Hope prayed.
*With the days she has left, let her know love one more
time.*

Chapter Five

~

Matthew knew what his mother was up to the minute that he saw Hope through the Sunshine Café's front window.

"Look, there's Nora and her granddaughter." Mom flashed him a not-so-innocent smile. "I told Nora to get a table big enough for all of us. I thought brunch sounded like just the thing. I told Harold to meet us there, but it looks like Helen might be coming, too."

"Mom, tell me you didn't invite Hope and Nora to join us." Matthew kept tight hold on Ian and Kale as he stopped in his tracks in the middle of the sidewalk crowded with after-church traffic. "Tell me you wouldn't meddle in my life like that."

"It's just brunch. Nora's been so housebound I thought—"

"You didn't think. You just decided what you wanted to do and lied about it to me."

"Lied?" Her jaw sagged and her free hand lighted

on the back of his. "I did no such thing. I just didn't tell you—"

"The truth?"

"No, that Hope would be joining us." Mom looked so proud of herself, as if she truly believed she was doing what was best for him. "Well, look, Nora's waving at us through the window. It's too late to back out now, but if you want to—"

Matthew's jaw snapped tight. He hated it when his mother did this. She meant well, and he figured she didn't want him to be as lonely as she was, but that didn't mean she could break open his heart like this and make him remember everything he was missing.

"Daddy!" Ian complained loudly, tugging hard against Matthew's grip. "I wanna hamburger."

"Hamburger, Daddy," Kale demanded. "I'm hungry."

They went inside, but he didn't like it. The boys were already counting on devouring one of their favorite meals and he wouldn't disappoint them. Not that he could stomach his mother thinking that her plan was working.

"Look at those darling boys," Nora crooned, welcoming them all with a bright hello.

Hope sat at her grandmother's side, somehow elegant and country-fresh at the same time in a lavender cotton dress, the kind that swirled around her woman's form, making her look as tempting as spring. She met his gaze and shrugged, letting him know she'd been as tricked into this as he was.

"It's the lady!" Ian raced straight to Hope and climbed onto the empty chair beside her with a clatter.

Hope held the chair steady as the boy settled down next to her. "I like your shirt."

"Trucks." Ian looked down at his shirt and slapped his little hand across a red truck imprinted there. "This is a fire truck—" he moved his fingers "—and a ladder truck and a tanker truck."

Matthew hefted Kale onto a chair at the end of the table, leaving his mother to deal with the booster seats the waitress was lugging toward them, and went to rescue Hope.

"He's into trucks," Matthew explained as he bent to haul Ian out of the chair next to Hope, where he clearly didn't belong.

"So am I, as a matter of fact." She laid her warm fingers on his forearm to stop him from lifting the boy away, and her touch and words surprised him. "Ian, guess what? I saw a dump truck yesterday."

"I seed a fire truck and…and it had water and everything." Ian looked proud of himself.

Mom, at the end of the table, shot a happy look at Nora and beamed as if she'd discovered a big pot of gold.

"Okay, that's enough." Matthew grabbed Ian around the middle. Hope might be a good sport about his mother's meddling and she was being kind to his son, but she clearly wasn't into children. It wasn't as if, at her age, she was married with kids of her own. "Little fireman, let's get you over here with Gramma so you can't bother Hope."

"He can stay, Matthew." Her words were velvet steel. "If you want to move him, fine, but he's not bothering me."

"He'll be like this through the whole meal."

"I like Ian. He's a fellow truck lover." The truth shone in her eyes—she seemed to really want Ian beside her. "Look, if you don't trust me with him, sit right here with us and make sure I don't start a food fight."

"Are you kidding? Look at those two old meddling women." He looked up to find both Mom and Nora watching him.

"Watch who you're calling old, young man," Nora admonished but looked undaunted as she winked at him. "Look at how your little boy takes to Hope."

Help. That's what he needed. Big-time help. Before he could protest, Hope spoke up.

"Nanna, you know I like children, so stop torturing Matthew or I'll burn your supper tonight." Hope flashed her grandmother a warning look, but her words held no real threat.

The door behind him snapped open and Helen walked through, escorting Harold. As the older women turned to greet the newcomers, Matthew knelt beside Hope and lowered his voice. "If we don't protest this with a united front, they'll think their matchmaking tricks are working."

"So? Let them." There were shadows in Hope's eyes, too, and he watched her press a hand to her stomach, as if she were in pain. "Sooner or later they'll figure out the truth and they'll be happily married by then."

She looked confident and somehow unhappy, too, and that troubled him. He wasn't the only one hurt by this. As Helen and Harold made their way to the table, settling down on the far side of Nora, Matthew couldn't help leaning close to whisper in Hope's ear. "What about Helen?"

"Good question." She swept a lock of hair from her face, an unconscious gesture that drew his gaze, and he couldn't look away from her beauty. Her skin looked silken-soft, and she smelled like sun-kissed wildflowers.

Why couldn't he stop noticing?

Hope caught Matthew alone in front of the egg trays at the buffet server. Grabbing a plate, she slid into line behind him. "Those women are incorrigible, using little children to further their matchmaking plans. Look at them."

Matthew peered over his shoulder toward their table situated near the front of the café, where Patsy straightened up from pouring ketchup on Josh's plate. His mom flashed him a triumphant smile that might mean, "See, I was right." Seated next to Helen, Nanna laughed, caught in the act of spying.

"I see." He reached for a serving spoon, trying to control a building anger. "They look pleased with themselves."

"Too darn pleased."

"You're encouraging them." Matthew spooned a heap of scrambled eggs onto his plate. "And I don't like it. It's not like I want Mom to think there's a chance I would want—"

He paused. No, those words hadn't sounded right. That wasn't what he meant.

"Oh." Hope heard his words and her fingers knocked against a serving spoon with a clatter. "That's fine, Matthew. I'll straighten things out once we get back to the table."

He'd spoken without thinking, out of anger and hurt and frustration. "I'm sorry. I didn't mean I wouldn't want to be seen with you."

"It's okay. You have every right to your opinion." She scooped up a poached egg and plopped it on her plate, concentrating very hard so she didn't have to look at him. "I wasn't the nicest person in high school, I'll grant you that. But I was young and with the way my family behaved, I didn't know any better. That must be what you see when you look at me."

"That's not what I see." His gaze shot behind her to where customers were grabbing plates from the stack, and moved forward to the heated trays of crisp bacon and spicy sausages. "I meant, why would a beautiful woman who has everything want to hang out with me."

"Really, it's okay." Hope grabbed blindly for the tongs and dropped a bunch of sausages on her plate, then circled around Matthew, leaving him alone.

It wasn't okay, and she didn't know why, but a horrible tightness was squeezing into her chest. When she reached the table piled high with fruit and breads, she set her plate down and took a deep breath.

This was irrational. Completely insane. She should get a grip before someone noticed how upset she was. Taking a deep breath, she ladled melon slices onto her plate and tried not to take flight when Matthew eased beside her, reaching for a few sweet breads.

"Cinnamon rolls, for the boys." His shoulder brushed her arm as he arranged the sweet-smelling pastries onto his crowded plate. "Hope, I'm sorry. I just meant that it's not like either one of us wants half the town thinking we're together. Rumors spread fast in a small town."

"I see your point." Trying to hide her hurt, she released the spoon too quickly, and metal clattered against the glass bowl. "For your information, I'm not all that bad to be around, at least, I've had other people think so. I might not be the best person in the world but I'm not the worst, thank you very much.''

Without looking at him, even as he was opening his mouth to say whatever it was that would just make her angrier, she grabbed her plate and stormed toward the table, no longer caring who noticed.

''Have a nice chat with Matthew?''

Hope set the plate on the table in front of Nanna and glared at her grandmother. She caught Patsy with a withering look and willed her voice to be quiet but firm. ''No more matchmaking. I've had enough of it, and so has Matthew. Believe me, there's no chance in a blue moon that we'll ever have anything in common, so not another word. Not one more word.''

''She's right.'' Matthew towered behind her, square jaw clenched, broad shoulders set and a look of fury in his eyes. But his anger was controlled as he looked from his mother to Nanna, and then it seemed to fade away. ''You heard Hope. We're from different worlds and whatever you two have in mind is never going to work.''

''Don't they say that opposites attract?'' Patsy looked ready to launch into a full-out, charming defense but seemed to change her mind when she saw the look on her son's face. ''I only wanted to help, that's all. Look at these little tykes. They need a mother's care.''

''Yes, that's right, and we love you both. We want you to be happy.'' Nanna didn't look one bit sorry. ''Now, enough with this nonsense. Matthew, sit down and tend to your boys. Look what they've done with the ketchup.''

Matthew caught Kale before he wiped ketchup on his brother, distracted from the issue at hand, but

Hope wasn't fooled. She knew that Nanna had survived a life filled with losses and loneliness with an indomitable heart, and nothing would derail her, especially not something she felt was this important.

Frustrated, she kissed her grandmother's cheek and headed for the buffet table to fill a plate for herself. Her stomach burned and even if she wasn't hungry, she had to eat.

It wouldn't be easy, sitting next to Matthew's son and feeling Matthew's solid presence all through the meal…and maybe feeling his dislike of her.

There was no way he would ever make Mom understand. Matthew fought frustration as he opened the refrigerator and hauled out a yellow pitcher. He slammed the door and rummaged in the cupboard for a plastic glass.

Sure, Mom was sorry but she didn't understand. She thought he was lonely and that he was holding onto Kathy's memory so that he could keep his heart safe from the risk of loving again. Well, she couldn't be more wrong.

After pouring, he left the pitcher on the counter, snatched the glass and headed through the house. His footsteps echoed in the too-quiet rooms, and the dark shadows made him all too aware that he was alone. A wife would have turned on the lamps and maybe put on some soothing music. That's what Kathy always did. His heart warmed, remembering.

He switched on the lamps and shuffled through the CDs, but couldn't find anything that felt right. Silence was okay; he didn't need to cover up the sound of the empty hours between the triplets' bedtime and his own.

Matthew sat down in the recliner, put his feet up, drank some juice and grabbed the paperback book lying facedown on the end table. But when he flipped to where he'd left off reading last, the printed words stared back at him and he couldn't concentrate.

He kept seeing Hope storming away from him in the café, hiding her hurt feelings behind cool anger, and he slammed the book shut. Frustration and conscience tugged at him. He wanted to head outside and keep going until the darkness and the cool night air breezed away this horrible knot of emotion and confusion tightening around his heart.

As he launched out of the chair, his feet hit the ground with a thud and he flew across the room. The silence felt thunderous and the emptiness inside felt as endless as the night. The doorknob was in his hand and the next thing he knew he was pounding down the front steps and into the cool darkness.

The crisp winds lashed across him, tangling his hair and driving through his shirt and jeans. He shivered, but at least he was feeling something besides heartache. Besides loneliness.

The wind rustled through the maple leaves near the house, and the rattling whisper of the aspens along the property line chased away the silence still ringing in his ears. He breathed in the scents of night earth, grass and ripening alfalfa from the nearby fields at the edge of town as a distant coyote called out and was answered. An owl swooped close on broad, silent wings and cut across the path of light spilling through the open door. He missed Kathy so much.

Father, help me to put an end to this.

There was no answer from the night, no sense of calm, no solution whispering on the wind.

"Daddy?"

Matthew heard a sniff and spun around. Josh huddled on the doorstep, rubbing at his eyes with both fists, his spaceship printed pajamas trembling around his small form. "What are you doing out of bed, hotshot?"

"I'm thirsty."

"Then come have some water with me." Matthew scooped his youngest son into his arms and held him close. He headed back into the house, shut the door with his foot and carried Josh into the kitchen.

The boy didn't want to let go, so Matthew balanced him on one hip while he searched for a second glass and found a clean one in the top rack of the dishwasher. He filled the glass while Josh clung to him.

The small boy was too sleepy to talk. He drank, smacked his lips and closed his eyes. Matthew's heart tightened with love for his child. For Kathy's child.

With Josh's head bobbing against Matthew's shoulder, he carried his son down the hall to the dark bedroom where a Pooh Bear night-light cast a faint glow across the two other boys sound asleep in their beds, teddy bears clutched in small hands.

"Sweet dreams," Matthew whispered as he laid Josh down on the spaceship sheets and covered him with the matching comforter.

Josh murmured, reaching out. Matthew spotted the bear lying forgotten against the wall and pressed it against his son's chest. The boy yawned, eyes closed, and sleep claimed him. He didn't stir when Matthew kissed his brow.

Kathy would have loved this, tucking in the boys, basking in the peace and quiet. She would have treasured the sense of rightness, of a day well spent and the blessing of three healthy sons asleep in their beds. With every beat of his heart, he missed her.

She was no more than a blurred face in his mind, the distant memory of a kind voice, and maybe that's what troubled him most of all. The real reason he was on edge with his mother and had hurt Hope's feelings. Because his beloved Kathy was fading from his memory, a little bit at a time, leaving a void in his heart. He could no longer recall the exact tone of her voice or the exact shade of her blond hair. And her smile, her touch, her presence...

She'd been the love of his life, and she was fading away from him slowly, piece by piece, memory by memory.

Clenching his fists, Matthew stood, crossed the room and pulled the door closed behind him. The empty feeling of the house seemed to vibrate around him, and he knew what he had to do. He'd behaved badly today, and it tugged at his conscience like a fifty-pound weight.

After looking up the number in the white pages, Matthew punched the lighted buttons on the pad, glowing a faint yellow, and glanced at the kitchen clock. Not ten yet. Maybe she'd still be awake.

"Hello?" Hope's voice answered after the second ring, gentle as an evening breeze.

"It's Matthew. You have every right to hang up on me, but I wanted to talk with you. I need to apologize."

"It isn't important." A reserve crept into her words, now that she knew he was the caller.

"What could be more important than your feelings?" He waited while the seconds ticked by.

"Fine, apology accepted."

"Wait, give me a chance to actually apologize. And there's something I wanted to talk about with you—"

"Good night, Matthew." There was a click and the line went dead.

It was worse than he'd thought. Hope was truly angry with him. You sure handled that just fine. Did he call her back and tell her what Harold had told him today?

The static on the line seemed to answer him, and he dropped the receiver into the cradle. The night, the shadows and the loneliness remained, and now he could add being a horse's rear to the list.

Troubled, he paced through the house, locking the doors, checking the windows, turning out the lights, feeling empty inside. A verse came to him, quiet as the night. *So if you are suffering according to God's will, keep on doing what is right, and trust yourself to the God who made you, for He will never fail you.*

The frustration and pain raging inside him eased, and he no longer felt alone in the dark night. *Father, I'm struggling. Please show me the way.*

Nanna looked old, older than Hope had ever seen her. Bright, fresh morning light teased at the window and tossed lemony rays across the foot of the old four-poster bed. Heart heavy, Hope lifted the breakfast tray laden with untouched food as Nanna curled on her side, pale with pain and still from the effects of the medication.

"She overdid it yesterday." Kirby tried to reassure Hope in the kitchen, where she sat at the table bent over her paperwork. "Nora isn't young anymore, and an injury like this is hard on a woman her age. Try not to worry so much. The new dose of painkiller seems to be working, so let's hope she sleeps through the morning."

Hope prayed that Kirby was right as she filled the coffee carafe at the sink, the spray of water into the empty container ringing in her ears. She shut off the faucet and looked down at the smooth, shiny handles Matthew had installed, and the worry eased away, which made no sense because she was still angry at the way he'd treated her in the restaurant. His behavior toward her had been so different from when he'd helped her to the top of the McKaslin's barn roof, when he'd held her safe and kept her from stumbling.

He didn't want his sons near her, and he didn't want to be seen in the same café as her. Well, that was perfectly fine. She wasn't looking for a man, especially not a settling-down widower with three kids in tow. Really, that's not what she was looking for. And it didn't matter how cute those little boys were. Not one bit.

She didn't need a family. She didn't need love. She didn't need to start seeing a fairy tale where none could ever exist. At least, fairy tales didn't happen to her and she was wise enough and old enough to know it.

After spooning ground gourmet coffee into the filter and turning the coffeemaker on, she grabbed an old knife and headed outside. The sweet gentle warmth of morning breezed against her as she hopped down the steps. She then knelt alongside the flower bed that ran the length of the house.

Untended since Nanna's injury, weeds were taking a firm hold in the rich soil. Tulips vied with dandelions and thistles, and Hope vowed to do some weeding, maybe later today when Nanna was doing better. The thought strengthened her, but even as she cut flowers, her mind kept drifting back to Matthew Sheridan and her heart clenched.

Yesterday, as he worked to keep his little boys from playing with their food, he'd handled them with tenderness and patience. Something she wouldn't have thought a man, even one as good as Matthew, could have possessed. And this was the man who hadn't wanted her befriending his boys, and the man who didn't want half the town thinking he was with her.

Good, fine, get over it, she told herself. But part of her felt hurt and angry. Hurt because she wished he didn't look at her and see her mother's daughter. Angry because it was easier than admitting the truth.

She gathered the cut flowers, arranged them in a vase and carried them upstairs. Nanna slept on her side, one hand curled on her pillow, her gray hair swept back from her eyes making her look as vulnerable as a child.

Yesterday had been tough on Nanna, although she would never admit it. Hope had seen the look on her grandmother's face when Helen had walked into the café with her hand on Harold's arm. There had been a brief flicker of sadness and regret, and then she'd invited Helen to sit down next to her. Nanna had let go of her hopes, just like that, for the sake of her lifelong friend.

There had to be a way to make her happy. But what? Feeling lost, Hope scooted the vase onto the edge of the nightstand and nudged it into place, bumping into a gold-framed photograph.

Hope's heart melted when she saw her grandfather's picture, a man she'd met only twice as a child, and Nanna's love. They'd met in grade school, Nanna told her, and they played together in the creek that bordered their family's properties.

He'd been her true love, one that didn't fade even after his death. Nanna had been newly widowed when Hope had visited the year she'd turned seventeen—it felt so long ago now, but the memories filled her with emotion. She remembered how two females, one old and one young and both hurting, forged a bond of love that summer.

She looked at the kind man in the photograph, taken at a summer picnic, maybe the town's annual Founder's Days celebration. It was easy to recognize the love in Granddad's eyes as he danced with a younger Nanna beneath an endless azure sky.

For the first time, Hope let herself consider that maybe Nanna meant what she said about love. That sometimes, it was honest and true. It didn't hurt or belittle but made the whole world right.

Sometimes.

With Kirby's words of warning, Matthew negotiated the narrow staircase as quietly as he could in his work boots. A few boards squeaked as he reached the top, and he felt odd prowling down the hall, drawn by the splash of light through an open doorway.

No sounds of conversation came from the room at the end of the corridor. No soothing music or low drone of a television broke the stillness. There was only Hope perched on a chair at her grandmother's bedside, head bowed as she read from the Bible held open on her lap, the light from the window pouring over her shoulder to illuminate the pages.

In the span of a breath, he saw the depths of her heart as she turned the page, searching for passages. Every opinion he'd formed of Hope Ashton faded like fog in sun.

"Matthew," she whispered, startled, and closed her Bible with quiet reverence. "What are you doing here?"

He gestured toward the bed, where Nora barely disturbed the quilt. "I have the cabinets."

"Now isn't the best time." Hope laid her Bible on the crowded nightstand and padded across the wood floor as quietly as she could manage. "Where's Kirby?"

"Downstairs on the phone speaking with the doctor," he explained once they were in the hallway. "She said her call might take a while and that you might be up here all morning, so if I wanted you, I'd better fetch you myself."

"She's right." Hope led the way down the hallway. "I wouldn't be able to bribe you into coming back another day, could I?"

"If it's a good enough bribe," he teased, wishing he could mend how he'd hurt her.

She almost smiled, but it was enough to chase the lines of exhaustion from her soft face. When they reached the bottom of the stairs, the bright morning light accentuated the bruises of exhaustion beneath her eyes and surprised him.

He followed her through the front door and onto the wide old-fashioned porch where flowering vines clutched at the railing. The morning's breeze tossed back the dark curls escaping from Hope's ponytail and ruffled the hem of her T-shirt.

It was only then he realized what she was wearing—an old T-shirt with the imprint faded away and a stretched-out neck, and a pair of old gray sweatpants with a hole in the knee. She ambled to the old porch swing on stocking feet and sighed as she eased onto the board seat.

"Rough night?" he asked.

She nodded, this woman who could have hired a legion of nurses to take care of her grandmother. But she had come herself without nurses or help from the rest of her family. By the looks of it, she'd spent most of the night at Nora's side.

"I know what that's like. I didn't get a whole lot of sleep during the triplets' first two years." He headed toward the steps. "I better leave so you can get some rest. We'll worry about the cabinets some other time."

"I hope this doesn't mess up your work schedule."

"Don't you worry about my work. Since I finished the McKaslins' barn, I've got a few roofing jobs to do, but I'm always waiting on deliveries. I'll just give a call when I've got time and head on over. When Nora is feeling better, that is."

"I'm determined to feel optimistic—she's going to be fine." Hope offered him a weary smile. "You don't have to run off, you know. At least not before I get a chance to apologize."

"I'm the one who owes you an apology. I practiced it on the drive over here." He leaned against the rail, arms folded over his chest. "I gave you the wrong impression at the café."

"No, I understand. You've told me how you feel about your mom's matchmaking schemes, and I shouldn't have expected you to just shrug them off. You're right, we shouldn't encourage them."

"Now wait a minute. I was going to say that you were right. That those two stubborn opinionated wonderful women can matchmake all they want, but it won't do a bit of good. They can't influence us. And if you can have enough grace and class not to be obviously insulted that my mom would try to marry you off to a working man like me, then I can do the same."

"Yep, spending time with you has been torture. And those boys." Hope managed a weary smile, but emotion glinted like a new dawn in her eyes and told him what her words didn't. "Those sons of yours are the cutest kids I've ever seen in my life."

"You won Ian over. He loves a woman with truck knowledge."

"I'm a working-class woman, so I've seen a lot of trucks in my day." She glanced at him, chin up and gauntlet thrown.

"You're not a working-class woman, Hope. Not with your family's income bracket."

"I was never a part of that family." Her chin inched a notch higher. "I make my own way in this world."

"So, that explains the outfit."

"What?" Then she looked down at the battered pair of gray sweats with a gaping hole in the right knee and the white, so-old-it-was-graying T-shirt. "A true gentleman wouldn't have said a word, but you had to, didn't ya?"

"I'm tarnished around the edges."

"No kidding." Half-laughing, she swiped the stray curls that had escaped from her ponytail with one hand. "Who needs makeup, presentable clothes and combed hair, right?"

"It's like seeing you in a whole new light." The old impressions of the remote, pampered girl he'd known in high school and the expectations he'd had of a rich woman fell away, shattered forever. "It's not bad from where I'm standing."

"Sure, try to make me feel better. Yikes, I need a shower and, wow, I can't believe I look like this." Embarrassed, laughing at herself, she hopped to her stocking feet, leaving the swing rocking. "I have to go and…and…do something, anything."

"You look the best I've ever seen you." Maybe he shouldn't have spoken his heart, but it was too late, and Hope stopped her rapid departure.

She turned, and he saw again the woman seated at her grandmother's bedside, head bowed over the Bible in her lap. The exhaustion bruising Hope's eyes and the comfortable clothes she wore to care for an old woman through the night made her all the more beautiful to him.

"Tell anyone about this, and I'll deny it," she said.

"So, you *are* worried about your reputation, after all."

"You bet, buddy. Guess what your mother will assume if you tell her that you got a good glance at my bare knee?"

"It's not a bad knee," he confessed, but before she could answer Kirby stepped into sight and whispered something to Hope.

Alarm spread across Hope's face, chasing away the smile until only worry remained. "I have to go, Matthew."

"Is there anything I can do?"

Hope's gaze latched onto his, filling with tears.

"She's in a lot of pain, and the doctor isn't certain that the fracture is healing. Prayer would be a help."

"You've got it." Chest tight, Matthew watched her spin with a flick of her ponytail, and she was gone. Leaving him feeling both lonelier and more alive than he'd been in what felt like a lifetime.

At sixteen minutes before noon, Hope heard a car rumble down the long gravel drive. Patsy Sheridan climbed out into the brisk spring sunshine and, leaving the triplets belted into their car seats, carried a steaming casserole to the front door.

She'd handed the meal over to Kirby before Hope could make it downstairs, but the gratefulness washing over her didn't diminish after Patsy's car drove out of sight.

Later, flowers arrived and cakes and Helen brought supper by, a potluck favorite that was always the first to go at the church's picnics, according to Kirby.

As the dusk came, bringing shadows and evening light, Hope knew that in all her travels, all the places she'd been and photographed, home was here in Montana, in this small town where neighbors took care of one another.

She knew who to thank. Matthew Sheridan had spread the word of Nanna's relapse. And she owed him the world.

Chapter Six

"Is that Matthew's truck?" Nanna leaned toward the edge of the bed, fighting to see out the window.

"Hey, careful." Hope gently caught Nanna's elbow. "All we need for you is to fall and break another bone."

"I may have broken my leg, but I'm not fragile." Nanna nodded with satisfaction as Matthew's dark red pickup gleamed in the sun in the driveway below. "At least, not anymore. This bone will heal, or else. I've lost nearly a week in this room, and it's time to get a move on."

"Just remember what your doctor said, Nanna." Hope reached for the hairbrush and knelt on the floor, gently swiping the smooth-bristled brush through Nanna's soft cloud of gray hair. "Want me to braid this for you?"

"I'd love it, dear heart. I'm in a festive mood, as long as young Matthew Sheridan can get my cabinets right."

Hope bit her lip so she wouldn't smile. Fretting

over the cabinetry work might give Nanna something
to think about other than her injury. "I don't know if
I'd trust Matthew. He's one of the only carpenters in
town. Without much competition, how good can he
be?"

Nanna's eyes sparkled. "So, you like him, do
you?"

"Keep dreaming."

"A girl's got to try." Nanna fell silent, allowing
Hope to part and braid her hair, then finish the thick
French braid with a cheerful pink bow.

As Hope pulled a comfortable pair of clean pajamas from the bottom bureau drawer, the sound of a
second vehicle coming up the driveway drew their
attention.

Nanna tipped sideways again. "Goodness, that
looks like—"

"Harold." Hope couldn't believe her eyes as she
watched the distinguished-looking older man climb
from a restored 1950s forest-green pickup. A carpenter's belt hung at his waist as he headed for the back
door, his deep voice carrying as he greeted Matthew.

Was this what Matthew had tried to tell her on the
phone the night she'd been so abrupt with him? Hope
leaned against the window frame and felt the sun
warm her face. In the yard below, Matthew and Harold appeared, talking jovially as they unloaded the
heavy wood pieces from the back of Matthew's truck.

The sun gilded Matthew's powerful frame and
heaven knew, she shouldn't be noticing. A tingle
zinged down her spine, and a yearning she'd never
felt before opened wide in her heart.

"There's no way I'm going downstairs in these."

Nanna's two-piece cotton pajamas landed with a thunk on the end of the bed.

Hope turned from the window. "Nanna, have you ever thought about falling in love again?"

"Goodness, child, a woman my age doesn't waste what's left of her days wishing for romance. You have the greatest happiness life has to offer ahead of you. Marriage and children. Now don't lie to me, you have to want children."

Hope felt the warmth inside her wither and fade at the word *marriage.* Her stomach burned at the memory of exactly what that word meant to her, the old ulcer always remembering. Endless battles, bitter unhappiness and her parents' habitual neglect of her.

She tried to put the memory aside of the unhappy child hiding in the dark hallway, listening to the hurtful words her parents hurled at each other as if they were grenades. Fearful that this argument would be the one to drive Dad away.

And it reminded her of her own attempt at marriage, ended before it began. And her stomach felt as if it had caught fire. No, she wouldn't think about the time she was foolish enough to think that love could be real for her.

Determined to distract herself, Hope paced the sunny room. "Where's the shorts set I bought for you when we took that cruise last summer?"

"Try the drawer chest, second to the bottom."

Sure enough, the soft blue-and-pink print knit shorts and top were folded amid Nanna's summer wear, surrounded by sachets of sweet honeysuckle. As she helped her grandmother into the clothes, she wished Matthew had told her he'd invited Harold over.

Kirby tapped down the hall and into the room and together they carried Nanna downstairs. "No, the garden," she insisted when they tried to situate her in the living room. "I need to feel the warmth of the sun on these old bones."

"Let me help." Matthew strode into the room like a myth—all power, steel and hero. He lifted Nanna into his strong arms, cradling her against his chest. "Nora, it's been a long time since I've held such a beautiful woman in my arms."

"That's a line you ought to use on my granddaughter, not on an old woman like me."

"I'm partial to older women."

Now I'm going to have to like him. Really, really like him, Hope thought as she held open the wooden framed screen door for Matthew. I've run completely out of excuses.

There was no turning back her feelings, especially when he set Nanna onto the shaded, wrought-iron bench with the same care he showed his sons. Tender, gentle, kind, he grabbed one of the matching chairs and drew it close. Watching him made that tingle zing down Hope's spine again.

No doubt about it, she was in trouble now. As she accepted the pillows Kirby had thought to fetch, she tried not to look at him, but he drew her attention like dawn to the sun.

"Are you going to give me that last pillow?" His mouth curved into a one-sided grin as she handed it over. "I'll have you ladies know that this service is entirely free. It won't show up on the bill."

"You're a real bargain." Hope tried to sound light but failed as he laid the pillow on the seat of a chair and lifted Nanna's leg into place.

Their gazes met and Hope heard the morning breezes loud in her ears. Awareness shot down her spine again.

His slow grin broadened. "I've been told that before. I never overcharge." He stood, towering over her, casting her in shadow. "But I do accept tips. Cash or baked goods."

He was kidding, but Hope couldn't smile. Kirby arrived with Nanna's Bible, reading glasses and the cordless phone.

They were shooed away by the old woman who thought she was matchmaking by sending them off to be together. "Take your time, Matthew. I don't need the cabinets today."

Hope shook her head, taking the lead down the garden path. "Sure, she's been fretting over the cabinets all week."

"That's all right, we'll fix her." Matthew's feet tapped on the flagstones behind her. "I brought Harold."

"I noticed. I thought he was interested in Helen."

"Helen is interested in him." Matthew caught her arm, stopping her before she could reach the back porch. "He avoided the subject when I asked him how he felt. All he would say is that he hardly knew Helen, that's all. I figure, until it's decided for sure, we might as well put him and Nora together and see what happens."

"Great idea, but you could have warned me."

"Harold didn't make up his mind until the last minute." Matthew's hand flew to his jeans pocket and withdrew a black pager, vibrating in his open palm. "It's Mom. Can I use your phone?"

"For a fee."

His grin was slow and stunning, and he darted past her, taking the porch steps in one stride, leaving her breathless.

She wasn't interested in Matthew Sheridan and he wasn't looking for marriage, but she couldn't help but wonder for the first time in her life what it would feel like to spend time with a man like him. To know the shelter of his arms and the tenderness of his kiss.

Gentle warmth spilled through her at the thought. What was wrong with her? Why on earth was she feeling this way? Hadn't she failed miserably at her one attempt to open her heart and hadn't she learned her lesson? That it was better to live alone and safe than give a man control of her heart?

Matthew reappeared, frowning, his hair disheveled as if he'd been raking one hand through it. "The job's off for this morning. Harold can't do the heavy work alone because of his bad back, and I've got to go. I can rearrange things for tomorrow afternoon. How about it?"

"What happened? Is something wrong with your boys?"

"No, not with the triplets." Matthew's frown deepened. "My mom's sick. She didn't look so good this morning, but she insisted she was fine enough to baby-sit."

"Of course, you need to check on her." Hope followed him down the path. "Is there anything I can do?"

"Yeah, find me a real good baby-sitter. One who isn't afraid of three little boys."

"That shouldn't be hard." Nanna spoke up from her serene bench in the shade. "Is something wrong, Matthew?"

"Mom's allergies are acting up and she isn't up to handling the boys." Matthew's brow frowned with concern.

Hope's heart twisted. He was a good man, one who cared for his family genuinely and selflessly. She tried to imagine her own father setting aside work for any reason, especially his family. "I hired extra nurses. If your mom needs any care—"

"No." Matthew dug in his pocket for his keys, loping down the path and onto the gravel. "It's nothing like that. Appreciate it, though. Her new medication is making her drowsy, and she's just not up to chasing after the boys."

Hope stepped after him, wanting to soothe away the worry on his face and the lines of hardship bracketing his eyes. "If you need someone to look after your sons for the day, I could do it. You could bring them here. Nora now has two nurses to take care of her and hardly needs me. I wouldn't mind keeping an eye on them."

"Nora needs peace and quiet."

"Let me go ask her. I—"

"Don't mind a bit," Nanna's voice called clear as a bell through the foliage that separated the driveway from the garden. "Doesn't Proverbs say that a cheerful heart is good medicine? Watching those boys of yours play will be all the cheer I need."

"No. Absolutely not." Matthew yanked open his truck door. "Hope, it's a nice offer, but you don't want to look after my sons."

"Why not? Ian and I struck up a friendship in the café, and I'm sure I can charm the other two."

"No. You're a…" He looked at her from head to toe and blushed. "You're a beautiful woman, and I can't see you getting down and dirty with three energetic little boys. You don't know what you'd be getting yourself into.''

''I saw them in action at Sunday brunch. They move fast, but I'm faster. Besides, Nanna needs some joy in her life, and something tells me your sons will keep her laughing.''

''You don't want to take care of these kids, trust me.''

But he was weakening, she could see it, and so she went in for the kill. ''Nanna really wants her cabinets finished.''

''Nora's been ailing. She wouldn't be able to get any rest.''

''She's listening to every word we're saying, so she'd speak up if that were true. Besides, I owe you a favor for all the wonderful things you've done for my grandmother and me. So consider this payback, got it? After this we're even.''

''It's a bad idea, Hope.'' Matthew raked one hand through his hair, leaving more dark strands standing up on end to ruffle in the breeze.

Hope fought the urge to reach out and smooth down those strands. Her hand tingled at the thought of touching him that way.

''You're not used to one kid, let alone three.''

''We have certified registered nurses on the premises. What could go wrong?''

Laugh lines crinkled around his eyes. ''You'll be sorry you said that, just wait and see.''

''Then it's decided.''

''Well...it would help me out. If you're sure.''

''Absolutely.''

Doubt lingered in his eyes, but his grin came easily.

"Fine. We'll just see how the morning goes first, then we'll see if you've changed your mind."

Long after he'd driven off, Hope still felt the tingle in her spine and warmth in her heart.

Kneeling in dirt in what would soon be Nanna's vegetable garden, Hope looked up as Matthew strolled onto the back porch looking as though he'd been working hard. His T-shirt and jeans were smudged with sawdust, and the carpenter's belt cinched at his hips was missing a few tools.

He squinted in her direction, his amusement as bright as spring. "You look exhausted. Are you sorry yet?"

"Give me ten more minutes, then I might be." Laughing, Hope ducked as a handful of dirt came flying her way. "Hey, Kale, I saw that. Lower that hand right now. *Right now.*"

As the boy reluctantly complied, tossing a look of warning to his older brother, whom he was aiming for, Matthew's chuckle rang out, effecting her from her head to her toes. "Boys, I told you no fighting."

"It's Josh's fault." Kale spoke up, always ready to pass the blame. "He's throwing."

"Nope, I'm talking to you, buddy." Matthew loped down the steps and moved a potted tomato plant out of the way. Then he crouched down, his gaze meeting Hope's across the span of freshly turned dirt. "I didn't know dump trucks and graders were useful in a garden."

"Of vital importance. Look how busy it's keeping them. For now." Hope laughed as Josh made a truck engine sound, content on leveling out the far end of

Nanna's unplanted garden. "How's the work coming?"

"The cabinet's in. I talked Harold into fetching Nora. Figured she'd want to see what I'd done before he starts the finishing work."

"I thought you two were going to do that work together."

"We were, until I lost Mom as a baby-sitter. I just called her and she's feeling better, but not well enough to take the boys."

"They can stay the rest of the afternoon, don't worry. You're not putting me out, and Nanna's getting a kick out of watching them. Ian took a worm he found over for her to praise, and she's still glowing. Over a worm."

"She's pining for great grandchildren."

"Count on it. She figures I'm her only hope." Longing speared her sharp as a new blade. Really, she didn't need a family. She didn't need a man in her life trying to dominate her and belittle her. Isn't that what most marriages were?

Ian dashed through the fragile rows of newly planted vegetables, carrying a bright yellow tractor. "Daddy, come see right now."

"Over here, Daddy." Kale hollered as he scooted a bright yellow dump truck into a rock with a clang. "Come see the big hole we dug."

"It's a huge one, Matthew, so be careful not to fall into it." Hope winked as she grabbed a six-pack of tomato plants.

Matthew watched her hands gently break apart the dirt and ease the first sprout into the rich earth. Her touch was gentle as she patted the dirt around the roots, and for one brief second he wondered what it would feel like to take her hand in his. Not in a quick touch to steady her on the barn roof or help her from the ladder, but to hold her hand, her palm to his, their fingers entwined.

He felt ashamed for even thinking of it. He was a man, he was human, and the Good Lord knew he was lonely, but this was the first time since Kathy's death he thought about another woman. Guilt cinched hard around his heart, leaving him confused.

Then Hope reached past him, brushing his knee with the edge of her glove as she grabbed one of the last tomato plants.

"You look at home here in the garden." Matthew couldn't seem to take his eyes from her. "There's dirt smudges on your face."

"Probably." She swiped her forearm across her brow and left another. "I'm a mess. Why is it that whenever you come over, I look like I've rolled out of a drainage ditch?"

"Lucky for you, it's a look I like. Especially the leaf in your hair."

"Oh, dear." She tore off one glove, revealing slender fingers stained with dirt.

"Here, let me." It was a simple thing, reaching forward and lifting the green half of a tomato leaf from her hair, but it felt as natural as if he'd been this close to Hope all his life. Already the floral scents of her skin and shampoo felt like a memory, and he knew, if he lowered his hand just a few inches to brush the side of her face, her skin would feel like warm silk against his callused fingers.

Guilt pounded through him with renewed force, and he let the leaf blow away in the wind.

"Daddy!" Ian stomped his foot, his voice hard with indignation. "Listen."

Oh, boy, how long had the kid been trying to get his attention? And how could he not hear his own son? "I'm coming, buddy."

He climbed to his feet, and Ian's small gritty fingers curled around his and held on with viselike force. He watched as Ian shot a jealous look at Hope. A lot of women who'd sacrificed their morning to watch over someone else's children might have taken offense, but Hope merely shrugged, her mouth soft with amusement.

It was there on her face, radiant and sincere, and he couldn't get it out of his head as he knelt in front of a small pit to praise the boys' busywork. She liked his boys, and he couldn't fault her for that.

"Matthew, look." Her whispered words as gentle as a spring breeze tingled over him and, at the look of hope in her eyes, his heart skipped a beat.

Harold was carrying Nora in his arms from the garden to the back porch. It was one of the sweetest things he'd ever seen.

"Daddy." Josh let go of his grader, and the truck tumbled to the ground with a clang. "I'm *real* hungry."

"Me, too!" the other boys chimed.

"You've got to be kidding. It's ten-thirty in the morning. Nope, no food. I'm starving you three from here on out."

The triplets started demanding hamburgers, and Matthew watched Hope climb to her feet, brushing the dirt off her clothes.

"It will be after eleven by the time we get to town." She lifted her chin in challenge. "We can get take-out hamburgers and they'll be fueled up for the rest of the afternoon.''

"No way. I'm not imposing on you like that. You have Nora to look after.''

"She's a soft spot in my heart, and I let her stay up too long this morning. She's going to be napping all afternoon, believe me, so I'll have plenty of free time.'' Hope rubbed a smudge of dirt from her cheek with her hands, leaving another bigger smudge. "Besides, I have it on good authority that Nanna loves cheeseburgers. Even older women need their protein.''

"Hamburgers, hamburgers,'' the triplets chanted.

"All right, boys, you win. Let's get you in the truck. And you. Stop encouraging them.'' He shot a gaze at Hope, who was carefully treading through the rows of vulnerable new plants.

"Hey, I wanted hamburgers, too.'' The wind tousled the dark strands that framed her face.

His chest cinched tight, and he wished he could stop noticing how the sunlight sheened on her velvet hair and caressed the silken curve of her cheek.

But most of all, it was her hands that caught his attention, slim but capable-looking, sensitive but strong. Hands that had helped care for her ailing grandmother, hands that could coax beauty from a camera and hands that he wanted to take in his own.

But that was because he missed Kathy. That was the only explanation. The longing in his heart for a woman's touch was really the longing for Kathy's touch, forever lost to him. It wasn't an attraction to Hope.

"I'll help get the boys buckled in,'' she offered, following the triplets to the truck.

His heart cinched. A part of him knew that it wasn't Kathy he wanted to touch right now, and as Hope trotted away, offering to race the boys, he wondered what his feelings meant.

He'd asked the Lord to show him the way. Surely these feelings for Hope weren't God's answer to his prayers.

"I tried to seat them together," Matthew whispered as he climbed onto the picnic bench beside her, his breath warm against the outer shell of her ear. "Harold was stubborn."

"And look at Nanna, she's talking to Josh and completely ignoring Harold." Hope snatched an onion ring from one of the waxed paper boxes in the middle of the old weatherworn table. "We're dismal failures as matchmakers."

"Good thing we're not done yet."

"I'm glad you're not easily defeated, because neither am I." Not now that she realized how much her grandmother needed someone in her life, someone to love. And that's what she would concentrate on. "I know Nanna's interested in him, but you wouldn't know it to look at them."

"Kale, throw that fry and you won't get more," Matthew interrupted as one dark-haired little boy held a ketchup-tipped curly French fry in midair, contemplating the merits of lobbing it at Ian and losing his fry privilege completely.

Ian solved the dilemma by flinging a fry at Kale instead and splattering ketchup across the table.

"That's it, you boys have sat long enough." Matthew leaped up to prevent any more throwing. "Get up and run off that energy. And stay where I can see you.''

Two identical little boys hopped off the bench, legs pumping, sneakers pounding, tearing through the grass field behind the house. A small plane cut through the wispy white clouds in the blue sky above, and the boys spread their arms like wings, making plane engine noises.

''My, I'd forgotten what fun they are at that age. And so much energy!'' Nanna beamed with delight as she watched them. ''My son was just like that, always on the go, always thinking. About ran me ragged, he did. How you manage with three of them, I'll never know. It would take a special woman to be a stepmother to three three-year-olds.''

''Nanna, I think it's time for you to go upstairs.'' Hope snatched another onion ring from the basket and shared a conspiratorial smile with Matthew. He looked ready to set Nanna straight, ready to come to Hope's aid if she needed him.

Not that she needed him.

Matthew stood alongside her, scooped Josh from the bench and set him on the ground. The little boy raced off to join his brothers, arms spread, soaring through the fresh young grass waving in the wind. ''Harold, if you keep an eye on my sons, I'll carry Nora upstairs.''

''Sure thing.'' The older man nodded, pride at his great grandsons alight on his handsome face, before nodding politely to Nanna. ''You take care, Nora.''

''Oh, my granddaughter will see to that.'' There was no want, no coveting in Nanna's clear eyes as she smiled.

Hope ached for her grandmother. Harold seemed

as if he liked Nanna, and Hope fought disappointment as she took Nanna's hand.

"She looks too tired." Matthew appeared at Hope's side, his strong warm presence unmistakable. "Nora, come lean on me."

So it was with gratitude that she followed Matthew up the stairs as he cradled Nanna in his arms. The bedroom windows were open to the sun, and the lace curtains fluttered in cadence with the wind. The distant sounds of small boys' laughter and the hum of engines sounded merry and seemed to fill the lonely old house with a welcome joy.

Hope tugged down the top sheet and stepped back so Matthew could lower Nanna onto the mattress with tender care. Hope's chest swelled with more than gratefulness and she turned away as a warmth that had nothing to do with appreciation spilled into her veins.

"Bless you, Matthew." Easing back into her pillows, Nanna pressed her lips together to hide a moan of pain. Kirby rushed in with noontime medication and a glass of water to wash down the collection of pills.

Matthew took the older woman's aged hand in his and squeezed gently. "You take it easy now and rest. I can't thank you enough for allowing my boys to stay."

Nanna's eyes glistened. "They made this place feel happy, like it used to when my children were young. I can't tell you what it did for this old heart of mine."

Matthew eased back to give Kirby room to work, and Hope followed him into the narrow hallway, which was warm from the heat of the day. Feelings she couldn't name fought for recognition in her heart as she struggled with the locked window at the end of the hall. It wouldn't budge.

"Let me." Matthew's arm brushed hers as he took over, efficiently manhandling the stubborn old lock and lifting the equally obstinate wooden window.

The heat from his brief touch lingered on the outside of her arm and didn't go away, even when she stepped farther back, even when she rubbed at the spot on her arm. Was it her loneliness making her feel this way? She didn't like it, not one bit.

"Harold's going to go ahead with the finishing work. He's excellent at it." As if he felt it, too, Matthew backed away, creating distance between them, and his gaze locked on hers, warm and intimate.

Way too intimate. Panic leaped to life inside her. "I'm glad you're leaving the boys for the rest of the afternoon."

"It looks like you're managing." He caught hold of the banister and hesitated. "I'd like to stop by and check on my mom."

"Why don't you give her a call from here, and if she's still under the weather, I'll send home some food for her, so she doesn't have to cook tonight. The refrigerator is packed, thanks to your thoughtful words to the pastor."

"That's what friends are for." He tossed her a slow grin, one that lit up the hazel twinkles in his eyes.

"Is that what we are? Friends?"

"Why not, it's better than being enemies, or adversaries or afraid of the matchmaking women in our lives."

The confusion coiled in her chest eased. Yes, they were friends. And there was nothing she would like more. Friends were safe. Friends didn't demand a vulnerable part of your heart.

"Speaking of our matchmaking relatives, I'm going to need your help." She swept past him, careful not to brush against him, and skipped down the stairs. "I'm going to make a list of all the eligible men in your mom's age group. I don't know what to do about Harold. I know Nanna is still interested in him, but Helen is her best friend. That's the way Nanna is, and I love her for it. So we'll have to find her someone as nice."

"That's going to be hard." Matthew's step echoed in the kitchen behind her. "Look."

Hope eased the screen door open to get a better view of Harold running in the calf-high grass, arms spread, making airplane noises with his three great grandsons.

"I think we should leave it up to the Lord." Matthew's grin broadened, and he was handsome enough to make Hope's senses spin.

Somehow she managed to speak. "What about Helen?"

"'And we know that God causes everything to work together for the good of those who love Him.'" Matthew splayed both hands on the porch rail and squinted through the sun to watch Harold dive-bomb Ian, then pretend to have engine trouble and drop to the ground. The boys giggled. "We'll let Him work it out. Whatever's meant to happen will. I have a suggestion, though."

"I'm almost afraid to ask."

"I think Nora might be happy if Harold refinished every last one of her cabinets. Think how shiny and new they'd look."

"I like the way you think." Let Harold and Nanna spend time alone in this house, and if they were meant to be together, then the Lord would work it out in His own way. "Consider refinished cabinets my treat to Nanna. How about new linoleum and counter-tops?"

"I'm miraculously booked up, but I bet Harold might do it."

"Then we have a deal." She sidled up next to him at the porch rail, leaving enough space so their elbows wouldn't brush, and it felt good having a friend in Matthew.

She felt different, better than she could ever remember feeling.

Chapter Seven

The sun slanted low in the sky and thunderheads were gathering on the horizon in tall pillars of angry clouds by the time Matthew headed his pickup down Nora Greenley's drive. The tires crunched in the gravel, and the warm breeze from the open window blew against his face. It wasn't hot enough for air-conditioning yet, and with the approaching storm, the dusty air felt muggy.

He rounded the last corner and Nora's old white farmhouse rolled into view, a sprinkler casting arcs of water across the front lawn. The shade trees shivered in the gentle breezes as he pulled to a stop in the graveled area in front of the detached garage. He cut the engine, and the familiar sound of his sons' laughter came distant but welcome.

So, Hope had survived the threesome after all. Warmth gathered in his chest, an emotion he couldn't name as he hopped from the truck and strode down the garden path. The rich scents of pollen, blooming plants and new roses felt as mellow as the late afternoon light.

He rounded the corner of the house and stopped in his tracks at the sight of his boys racing around on the back lawn, squealing whenever Hope hit one of them with a blast from the garden hose. Drenched, Ian darted one way, Kale the other, and Josh got hit full-force in the stomach.

"It's cold!" he shrieked, face pink with delight.

"Catch me, Hope!" Ian waved both hands, then took off running the instant she turned the nozzle toward him. With a shout, Ian hopped away from the cold water jet, laughing as Hope took off after him, hose snaking in the grass behind her. Water sprayed over him, drenching him from head to toe.

"Gotcha!" Hope called victoriously, then quick as a whip shot water at Kale, who wasn't expecting it.

"Run, Kale, run!" Ian urged, and the three took off toward the garden gate, trying to outdistance the arcing geyser that was quickly catching up to them.

Then Josh spotted him. "Daddy! Daddy!"

"Daddy!" They headed toward him talking at once, their bare chests glistening in the warm sun and their brown locks sluicing water as they ran.

"Hope sprinkled us with the hose and not the grass," Ian shouted over his brothers. "It's real cold. We want pizza."

"Pizza, pizza!" the other two demanded.

"You boys have food on the brain." Matthew knelt down as they launched toward him and didn't mind their wet hugs one bit. "Ready to head home?"

"Is Hope comin', too?" Kale wanted to know.

"Hope has to stay here with her grandmother."

Matthew stood, and the tiny hairs on his arms and the back of his neck prickled when Hope padded close.

"I sure had a lot of fun with you three today." She'd rescued their shirts from the porch railing, and she held them out now. "Let me run inside and grab some towels. I'm afraid I got your boys a little wet."

"They're sweet, but they won't melt. Already tried it." He winked, and he liked the smile that shaped her face. His fingers brushed hers as he took the shirts, and for the life of him he couldn't stop looking at her.

She simply glowed, out of breath from chasing his boys, dripping wet, her hair tumbling in thick shanks, and he wanted to pull her close to him. To take her in his arms and hold her, simply hold her, as if her brightness could chase away the shadows inside him and make right every wrong in his world.

But he hesitated, knowing he had no right. There was too much to stop him.

The moment was lost, and she stepped away, heading toward the porch. "I'll be right back."

"Don't bother with the towels. They'll dry off in the truck. It's hot enough. Okay, boys, time to head out and give Hope some peace and quiet."

"Why?" Ian demanded. "Wanna get sprinkled by the hose."

Matthew recognized the signs. A long, exciting day and no nap. "Looks like I'd better get them home and fast. Thanks again for watching them."

"I hope it helped you out. Heaven knows you've done more than enough for me."

He couldn't look at her any longer, torn between the past and something that felt frightening to think about. "I was able to finish another job this afternoon. It made a huge difference."

"Good." A world of goodness shone in her eyes as their gazes met and held.

It felt like a deep chasm breaking his heart into pieces and he stepped back, searching but not finding words to begin to explain.

"Bye, boys," Hope called, lifting a hand, looking as attractive and beautiful as morning, and he wished....

A part of him wished.

The boys called out in answer, grumbling first, then telling him about every aspect of their afternoon with Hope. How she'd let them dig holes for the baby corn plants, how they'd watered the garden and got into a water fight, and the chocolate cookies she'd given them.

She'd taken their pictures, and they climbed trees and ran through the sprinkler until they were cold. Their happiness filled the cab of the truck but it didn't touch him as he first belted each boy in tight, then climbed in behind the steering wheel.

He could see Hope through the shivering leaves of the willows as she set the sprinkler in the backyard. Then the boughs moved, blown by a harsher wind, signaling the first edge of a storm and hiding her from his sight. But not from his mind.

Wishing, aware of a great emptiness in the deepest part of him, he headed down the road, straight toward the dark shadow of gathering angry clouds, already dreading the night ahead.

"I happened to see you and Matthew talking alone together," Nanna commented, patting the sheets smooth over her legs to make a place for the supper tray. "You two sure look like you're getting along well."

"Why wouldn't we? We're on the Founder's Days planning committee together, thanks to you and Patsy, so we have to find a way to cooperate. And what were you doing out of bed?" Hope set the tray into place and checked the wooden legs to make sure they were locked and sturdy. "Don't tell me you got up without anyone noticing."

"I could hear you two talking because my window is wide open." Nanna's bright eyes spoke of something more as she unfolded the paper napkin and spread it over her lap. "Sounds like those boys of his have really taken to you."

"They're nice boys, and I know where you're headed, so don't go there and say grace instead."

Nanna chuckled. "'Fools think they need no advice, but the wise ones listen to others.' I've told you before and I'll tell you again, you need roots, Hope. You're like me, and I watched you with Matthew's boys today. You had joy in your eyes for the first time since you've come back, and it makes my heart glad."

"I like children. I never said I didn't. You have to stop this pressure, Nanna. I know what you expect from me and what you want from me." Her stomach burned, and she could feel the day's lightness slipping away.

A great emptiness opened up inside her, an emptiness that hurt. How did a person know that love would last?

Love didn't come with guarantees.

Tucking away her fears, Hope decided to take

charge of the conversation. "Now say grace because I'm starving."

Over the pleasant supper, Hope steered far away from Matthew and made a point to ask about the people in town she'd known as a teenager and how they were doing now. Nanna's exhaustion caught up with her. Her nighttime medication put her to sleep before she had time for her prayers and chamomile tea, so Hope took the pot with her to the living room.

Wind whipped through the open windows, lashing the lace curtains without mercy. With the scent of imminent thunder and rain strong in the air, Hope wrestled with the stubborn, warped wood window frames and wondered how on earth Nanna had managed to strong-arm these windows for so long.

A spill of light through the archway from the kitchen filled the room with shadows, and Hope flicked on lamps, listening to the sound of her footsteps loud in the emptiness. Even though Brittany, the new nurse she'd hired from the agency in Bozeman, was busy with her paperwork at the kitchen table, Hope felt the solitude as keenly as a punch to her chest.

Maybe it was because she'd had so much fun with the boys today, watching over them and marveling at how three identical children could be so different. Somehow she felt lonely without their constant noise, energy and happiness.

The old house echoed around her as she dug through the rolltop desk in the far corner. How could Nanna stand this night after night, year after year? Distant thunder boomed and the wind gusted, knocking a lilac bough hard against one of the windows.

Finally, Hope found what she was looking for and

carried the small stack of spiral-bound paper to the wing chair in the corner. She eyed the phone sitting there and grabbed the cordless receiver from the kitchen since there was an electrical storm on the way.

She dialed the number, listened to the four rings and felt her smile the minute Matthew answered. "It's Hope. Do you have the boys in bed yet?"

"I've got them last-minute water and found a missing teddy bear. The light is out, the door is closed and so far I haven't heard anyone hollering for me." The rich warmth in his words spoke of his deep love for his boys, something that couldn't be mistaken, and chased away the shadows in the room.

"Any luck with a housekeeper yet?"

"I've put an ad in the Bozeman paper. Mom's been against it, but she can't keep up with those three forever and it's too much to ask her to do full-time." He sighed, a sound of pent-up frustration.

"I'd be glad to help out again, if you get in a bind."

"I can't impose on you like that. How's Nora feeling after a day with the boys?"

"Her spirits are high and that's got to make a difference. She looks better, but it's going to be a long road for her. She initially refused the option of surgery. You know how stubborn she is. Tomorrow I'm taking her to the doctor in Bozeman and we'll see what he says. They're going to run some tests and if there's no sign of bone growth, I'm going to talk her into surgery. She'll have no choice."

"I'll be praying for both of you."

"Thanks, Matthew." Outside the house, the wind gusted so hard, shrubbery slammed against the windows, and the sound of wood scraping and clawing at the glass gave Hope the shivers. She curled up in the wing chair. "I have the church directory in hand. Do you have time to go through it looking for eligible bachelors?"

"For Mom and Nora." His voice smiled. "Sure, I've got time for a good cause."

Clutching the receiver between her ear and her shoulder, Hope opened the well-worn booklet to the first page and scanned the names until she spotted a man listed singly, without family members. "How about Brad Birch?"

"He's twenty-something."

"Okay, I'll cross him off the list. How about…" She ran the ballpoint pen down the page. "Austin Chandler?"

"He was a few years ahead of us in school." Matthew laughed. "Try again."

"Dr. Andrew Corey?"

"Hey, he's Mom's age." Across the wire came the sound of rustling, as if Matthew was looking for paper and pen. "I think they went to high school together."

"This is going to work, it has to. Patsy and Nanna are still young, considering. They shouldn't have to spend the years they have left alone. How about Zachary Drake? Wait, he's too young. Joseph Drummond?"

"Put him on your list."

Ten minutes later, Hope was staring at names of five lonely widowers, men who might be suitable for either Nanna or Patsy. "I have no clue what to do next. I've never done this before."

"Leave it to me. Got anything going on Saturday?"

"No real plans. Why?"

"It's a surprise." The deep rich timbre of his voice rumbled with expectation. "I'll pick you up at around eleven. Oh, and Hope? Wear sneakers."

"Sneakers? What are you up to? I won't necessarily need sneakers to hunt down the men on this list."

"You'll have to live dangerously and find out."

Laughing, she leaned back in the chair cushions and stretched her legs out, propping them on the corner of the coffee table. "Do I need to bring anything else?"

"Just your lovely self. Good night, Hope."

"Good night."

And then he was gone, the line went dead and the shadows returned.

"Are we there, Daddy?" Ian's question filled the cab of the pickup like a thunderclap. "Are we, are we?"

Matthew snatched a brief glance at his son in the rearview and couldn't hold back a grin. Hope had sure won over his boys. "We're almost there."

"But I wanna see Hope!" Kale complained, and Josh nodded in grave agreement.

"I'm turning into her driveway this very minute." Dust kicked up from the gravel road. The storm earlier in the week had dropped a bucket load of rain, but there was no sign of it now. The countryside shone green and gold from the distant hills to the fields on either side of the road, where tall grass waved in the temperate winds.

The minute his truck shot around the last curve, he spotted Hope sitting on the front porch next to her grandmother on the old wide-benched swing. The way Hope lifted her hand in greeting made him glad he'd invited her along.

"Hope! Hope! Hope, we saw a hay truck," Ian shouted, then was drowned out by his brothers. Three boys strained against the confines of their car seats to get Hope's attention.

"Hi, boys, Matthew." She rose from the swing and her gaze snared his, but there was only a flash of friendliness there. A warm, sweet friendliness. She turned to kiss her grandmother on the cheek, an equally sweet gesture, and the love and concern on her face left no doubt how grateful she was for Nora's slow improvement. "Nanna, I can still stay, if you need me."

"Goodness, I've got twice as many nurses as I need and an afternoon with nothing to do but feel the breeze on my face." Nora still looked pale, but the sparkle was in her eyes. "Go have some fun. It's past due."

"I'll make sure she does have some fun." Matthew called out his window and earned another one of Hope's smiles. "Nora, you're looking better."

"Nonsense, but I *am* feeling better," answered the spry woman, frail but determined, with her casted leg propped up on a stool. "The doctor said my bone is healing just fine and in another week I'm going back to my crutches, no matter what a certain pushy granddaughter of mine says. So you do me a favor and make sure my Hope relaxes, will you? She's worked herself to the bone the last few weeks, and it's time we put an end to it."

"Like I can't take care of myself, Nanna. Really." Hope skipped down the steps, the hem of her untucked cotton shirt fluttering around her waist and hips as she moved.

Matthew tore his gaze away and hopped from the truck. "Nora looks like she's happy about this outing of ours."

"Sure she does. She thinks we're going out on a date." With a wink, Hope accompanied him around the tailgate to the passenger side. "I heard her say that to your mom on the phone last night."

"You were eavesdropping?"

"No, but I heard her anyway. Don't worry, I didn't let her get away with it. I changed the subject to the list of eligible men at church, and I got a few clues."

He opened the truck door for her and held out his hand. "It's a step up. Here, let me help."

"I've climbed into your truck before," she argued but surprised him by placing her hand on his. Her touch was warm, her presence captivating and when he breathed in, he smelled the sunshine fragrance of her hair.

With the sun hot on his shoulders and a strange tingling down the back of his neck, he helped Hope into the truck and shut the door. Through the open window he could hear the boys yelling over each other, trying to win her attention.

As he circled around the hood, he watched Hope twist around in the seat and heard the velvet gentleness of her voice as she spoke to them. By the time he'd slipped behind the wheel, the boys had quieted down and were talking in turns about the trucks they'd spotted so far today.

Hope made a bet she could see more trucks than they could. Through the entire drive to Harold's ranch, shouts of "logging truck" or "gas truck" or "milk truck" peppered the air until Matthew joined in, spotting a coveted fire truck ambling along the country roads.

"Like picnics?" Matthew asked after he'd pulled off the paved road and onto a narrow dirt lane.

"Love them."

"Good, because I hoped you might take it in stride. Believe it or not, I thought you might like to see something of Montana, considering the pictures you take for a living and all." He braked and killed the engine. "Now I know this isn't an Italian countryside, but it's not bad."

"I guess not." She gazed ahead to the tall rim of white-capped mountains in the distance, jagged proud peaks spearing the forever-blue sky. "I hear a river."

"The Gallatin. Runs all the way from Yellowstone Park to the Missouri headwaters." This had always been his weekly retreat with the boys, and it felt right including her, this woman who had everything but seemed lonely in many ways. He knew a thing or two about loneliness.

"Want out, Daddy!" Kale demanded.

"Is Grampy Harold comin', too?" Josh asked.

"I'm hungry!" Ian announced, and Matthew knew there'd be no peace unless he unleashed his sons and let them run around in the sun and grass.

"Stay where I can see you," he warned Ian as he swept him from the car seat and let him go. "Kale, you, too."

"'Kay, Daddy." As soon as Kale's sneakers hit the ground, he was off to join his brother, who was running through the tall grass.

"Hurry, Daddy!" Josh squirmed in his seat and

made it harder to unbuckle him. The minute he was free, he tore off toward his brothers.

Matthew grabbed the picnic basket, and Hope was beside him, dark eyes laughing as she watched the boys burning off energy. His chest felt too tight to breathe. "Come on. I'll show you the river."

She smiled, and he felt its warmth all the way to his toes. His step seemed lighter as he herded the boys toward the copse of cottonwoods hiding the bank from sight. As she walked beside him, he heard her step in the grass, felt the whisper of the wind between them and heard the gentle rhythm of her breathing.

Her presence, her scent, her being felt so female, so womanly. She filled his senses, making his heart twist and ache. The emptiness inside felt too much to bear. He would miss Kathy, he would always miss her. But right now, he realized he was missing something even more.

"Oh, Matthew." Hope froze in her tracks, face lifted to the beautiful peaks in the background, taking in the simple rugged beauty of the river that winked with quiet confidence in the midday sun.

Across the wide river, a fragile antelope lifted her white muzzle from the water and studied them. The fawn at her flank stared hard at the boys, then in a flash both mother and baby leaped into the grass and disappeared.

The wind, the sweet-smelling fields, the powerful river and the mountain's beauty couldn't hold his attention the way Hope did. The awe on her face showed as she spun around slowly, gazing upstream at the beavers working in the waters of a nearby creek that emptied into the river. At the distinct white face and hooked yellow beak of the American eagle soaring overhead on a hunt, black wings spread in a breathtaking glide. And then at the river cutting its path through the rich Montana earth and clay, a deep silent force.

Hope breathed the words. "It's a different kind of beauty, wild and simple, better felt than seen."

Matthew merely nodded, his throat tight, captivated by this woman who made her living photographing sunsets in French vineyards or the play of light in the remains of a medieval cathedral. He knew without asking that she understood what he saw here—endless peace, the ever-turning circle of time and God's hand in the world.

"How would I capture this wind, I wonder?" Her hand lighted on the top of her camera case, but she didn't open it. "Or the feel of this river?"

"I'd planned on taking you downstream. Harold keeps a boat not far from here. He's a serious fisherman, but I don't like to mix three-year-olds and fishhooks."

"I can't imagine why."

Before he could answer, the boys charged toward them, their calls carrying on the wind, waving the sticks they'd just found high in the air.

"I got one for you." Josh handed the dry length of what had been once a tree branch to Hope. "The bestest one."

"Thanks, Josh." Hope knelt to take the gift offered with three-year-old pride. "You are a thoughtful boy."

He gave her a beaming grin before he took off with his brothers to try to get inside the picnic basket Matthew carried. But Matthew was slow to lift it out of their reach because he was too busy watching Hope hold that length of wood as if it were a treasured gift.

"It's not every day a girl gets a stick as good as this one," she told him with a smile that dazzled, that reached down to the chasm in his heart and warmed him like spring sunshine. "Your boys are acting like they're about to keel over from starvation."

"Thirsty, Daddy!" "I'm hungry, Daddy!" "Kale's pushin' me!" The words rang with deafening force, but Matthew moved by rote, sending the boys to pick out a picnic spot in the dappled shade.

All he could think of, see, hear and feel was Hope as she helped the boys settle the dispute over where to sit, with the wind in her hair and the sunlight caressing the soft curve of her face.

The way he longed to do.

Chapter Eight

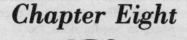

Hope bit into the cold chicken thigh and moaned. Crispy, moist, seasoned just right. "Did Patsy make this? It's delicious. I'm going to have Nanna ask for the recipe."

"Well, she's going to have to ask me because I made it." Across the blanket, above the boys' chatter, with the food spread out between them, Matthew spooned a generous helping of potato salad onto his paper plate. "Everything you see here, I did, and I'll be glad to share the recipe with a woman as beautiful as you."

"Compliments will get you everywhere." She laughed, feeling more at ease with her friend, and her opinion of him rose another notch. From what she could see, he was everything that a father should be.

When the boys got into an argument, he quieted the situation with kind words and a fair solution. When they were on the brink of a potato salad flinging fest, he stopped them with a word that was firm and not threatening. Love shone in his eyes whenever he looked at his boys.

It was so easy to see the depths of this man's heart, and she knew that's why she liked him. Why, when she'd spent her adult life avoiding any kind of relationship with a man other than in her work, she felt safe at Matthew's side—as his friend.

"Piggyback ride, Daddy!" Ian demanded, after finishing two helpings. His two brothers eagerly abandoned their plates to beg for rides, too.

"Okay, but don't wear your old dad out." Amid cheers, Matthew scooped Ian from the blanket and swung the boy onto his broad shoulders.

"Go, Daddy, go!" Ian chanted before he broke into laughter as Matthew raced through the knee-high grasses. "Faster! Faster!"

Hope snatched her pocket-size Nikon from her camera bag, uncovered the lens and focused. Frame by frame she caught Matthew's easy lope through the fields, the blue bunch wheat grass snapping against his tanned knees, scattering butterflies and startling larks.

Through the eye of the camera she caught the easy intimacy between father and son as Ian lifted both hands in the air, fingers extended as if trying to touch the sky. And then how he hugged Matthew hard, his arms banding around Matthew's forehead. Behind them stretched the vastness of crystal blue sky and puffy white clouds and the snow-capped Bridger Mountains, purple-blue and breathtaking.

With a final click, Hope captured father and son, profiles matching, dark shanks of hair tumbling over identical brows as they laughed, facing the wind.

"We wanna ride now!" Kale complained.

"I'm always last," Josh sighed to her.

Okay, she was a pushover. Every stray cat she'd ever come across had her pegged. And so did Josh as he toddled over the wrinkles in the blanket and reached out for her camera with sticky hands.

Too quick for him, Hope tucked it back into her bag. "I can give piggyback rides, too."

"You can?" Twinkles just like Matthew's sparkled in Josh's hazel eyes. "And run fast, too?"

"Just as fast as your daddy." She knelt, giving him her back. "Climb on."

Hot sticky fingers caught hold of her neck, tugging on a few strands of her hair. Then a knee dug into the middle of her right kidney. Hope reached around and gave Josh a boost, and his legs swung one at a time into place over her shoulders.

"Hold on tight, and we're good to go." As soon as she felt Josh's hands on her neck, she stumbled to her feet.

"Faster!" Josh squealed in her ear.

Hope caught hold of his shoes, holding him steady as she broke into a jog through the fragrant grasses. Josh was a sweet weight on her shoulders, bouncing and giggling with glee.

"I'm not last, Daddy!" he shouted with jubilation as Hope sprinted past him.

"Hey, wait a minute!" Matthew's back had been turned, and the surprise on his face transformed into an approving wink. "I'd race you, but I'd win."

"Don't count on it." She took off into the wind, pushing hard.

"We winnin', Daddy!" Josh twisted backward to shout, nearly throwing Hope off balance.

She managed to keep him right side up on her

shoulders, but Matthew took advantage and sprinted alongside her.

"You're pretty fast, Hope." He wasn't winded yet, and there was a challenge in his eye as he paced her. "I'm faster."

"You sound a little too confident to me." She leaped over the remains of a dead limb, and Josh shouted his approval.

Matthew sailed over the thick cottonwood bough, his gait smooth and steady. Kale's shouts spun Matthew around, and he stopped. Hope waited, too, as the third boy raced after them. "I want up now, Daddy! Please, please!"

Matthew knelt to let Kale crawl up behind Ian and somehow settled one on each shoulder. The boys seemed used to it, holding on tight, their heads leaning together to touch at the brow, their grins identical, and Hope's fingers itched for her camera.

"I'll race you back to the river. How about it?" Matthew's challenge was answered by the boys' shouts.

"I'm ready if you are."

His half grin turned saucy, as if he already figured he was the winner. "Ready? Go!"

He waited half a beat before taking off, and Hope leaped ahead of him. Let him try to be a gentleman, he was still going to lose. But the added weight of two boys didn't seem to slow him down any, and she fought to stay ahead of him as they swung along the fence line and headed straight for the river.

A hawk lighted on a post, took one look at them and soared skyward, wings spread, so majestic Hope longed to turn and watch the beautiful creature, but she didn't dare take her gaze from the ground. A prairie dog poked up from its home in the earth, chattered as if scolding them and ducked.

Matthew sailed over the hole, gaining on her. He was at her side, breathing hard, working to pass her. She wouldn't let him.

Shoulder to shoulder, neck and neck, they raced side by side, the boys urging them on. Matthew started pulling past her, running all out, breathing hard. Gasping for air, reaching down for the last bit of strength, she pushed past him and soared beyond the blanket's edge. She'd won!

"I can't believe it!" Matthew dropped to his knees, letting the boys tumble off his shoulders and into the grass, giggling.

Breathing hard, Matthew stretched out on the sun-baked grasses. "You're pretty good for a city girl."

"You're not bad for a country boy." On wobbly legs, she lowered herself to the ground. Josh dove off her shoulders into the soft grass, rolling around with his brothers. Out of breath, she sank back into the sweet fragrant grasses and stared at the sky, the exact color of a robin's egg.

Sunlight shot in streamers through the trailing wisps of cotton white clouds. High overhead were the twin tracks from an airplane, and if she squinted she could barely see its silver body flitting across the face of the sky.

"Daddy! Look." Kale stood up, pointing toward the far end of the blanket.

Hope watched Matthew roll on his side. "Why, you little thief. Get away from our basket." He climbed onto his feet, unfolding easily to his six-foot height. "Hey, those are our brownies."

Hope twisted around to see two little prairie dogs

trying to help themselves to something inside the basket. They looked up defiantly as Matthew loped toward them, then settled for stealing a biscuit before scurrying back to their home in the grass.

"Can you believe that? A guy's brownies aren't safe anywhere, I guess."

"Maybe we'de better eat them now so they aren't temptation for more wild creatures." Hope sat up and dusted grass from her hair.

"Good idea."

Already the three boys were helping themselves to the plate Matthew held out for them, taking a brownie in each hand. Anyone could see what a good man he was—no, what a great man he was. His humor and patience with the boys made her heart hurt in a way she couldn't explain and didn't much want to think about. They were friends. Just friends.

She inched over to her camera bag and tugged out the Nikon. She uncovered the lens and framed Matthew as he knelt with his boys, their adorable identical faces smeared with brownie frosting. The shutter clicked.

Matthew looked up, seeing her camera for the first time.

"I've been missing working, and I couldn't resist," she confessed. "You don't mind?"

"Nope. Not at all." He set the plate down between them and crouched with his back to the sun. "Now that you're sure Nora's leg is on the mend, will you be heading back to wherever it is you call home?"

"I have a condo in Malibu. And don't give me that look," she admonished as she stole a decadent-looking brownie from the plate. "It's a modest place, believe me. Just a one bedroom, something to call home, even if I'm hardly ever there.''

"Sure, well, I have a vacation home in Maui, but I'm hardly there, either.'' A slow jaunty grin tugged at the left corner of his mouth. "Will you be around to go to the Founder's Days dance with me?''

"Well, since we're two of the committee members, we might as well go together. Especially since your mom and my grandmother are expecting us to announce our engagement.''

"Mom was ecstatic when I let it slip I was seeing you this afternoon.''

"You saw the joy on Nanna's face when you drove up.'' Hope nibbled the edge of her brownie, and the rich chocolate sweetness melted on her tongue. "Whatever you do, don't let her know you can bake like this. I'll never hear the end of what a fine husband you'd make.''

"Hate to break your illusions about me, but this is from a box.'' He held up what remained of his brownie. "I'm really good at following directions, especially if they come with step-by-step pictures.''

He didn't know where it came from or how it happened, but one minute Hope was laughing and the next he had to fight to keep from claiming her mouth with a kiss. The need to hold her tenderly and cover her lips with his burned like a steady flame inside him.

Hope, unaware of his struggle, leaned on one elbow and lifted the camera. After a moment, the shutter clicked. "I think I found the angels in them, chocolate fingers and all.''

Her gentle humor wrapped around his heart and it only made him want her more. Shocked at himself and at his feelings, he hopped to his feet and rescued the empty plate from the ground.

"It's getting late." He couldn't look at Hope as he turned away. He just couldn't bear to look at her. "If we want to float down the river, then we'd better get going."

"Sounds like fun." By the sound of her voice, she had no idea what he was feeling and what he wanted from her. "Boys, let's get you cleaned up before we head out. Such a strong chocolate scent might bring out more than just the prairie dogs."

As she knelt down to do her best to wipe chocolate off the boys' faces, his heart broke open a little wider. She was like sunlight on summer afternoons, and how she warmed him.

Peace drifted on the winds and whispered in the swift deep waters of the Gallatin River. Hope drank in the beauty of the land sparse with trees but rich in wild beauty. The boys played with their bright green plastic fishing poles that sported no dangerous hooks, Matthew guided the boat by oar, and they drifted in the swift current. She slipped the camera out of her bag.

For the fun of it, she snapped shots of the boys and of Matthew, who merely shook his head at her, a dimple revealed in his left cheek.

"Don't you city girls know how to play?"

"I'm here, right?" How did she admit work was the only thing she had in her life, besides God? No one was waiting for her at home, no one missed her when she left town, and there was no one to hold close through the long nights. "This is my idea of fun. I know, amazing but true."

"Nora ordered me to make sure you relaxed."

"I *am* relaxed." She tilted her face to the sunlight and drank in the feeling of sun and wind and freedom against her skin.

"I've been hearing tales about you."

That drew her attention. Hope twisted around and settled into the curve of the bow. "Out with it. I want to know what you've heard."

"Afraid, huh?" He dipped the tip of one oar into the water and eased them along with the current. "I've heard a few things, actually. It seems quite a few people noticed the two of us together at the Sunshine Café for brunch after church that day. I've been asked by about four or five people just exactly what's going on between the two of us."

"Oh, as if we were there alone together instead of with our families."

"Exactly. From the sound of it, you'd think the two of us were having a romantic tryst." There was no sadness in his eyes as he met her gaze. "Don't worry, that particular rumor will die down. But there's another rumor I do believe that's being spread around this town and it's about you."

"I'm in trouble now."

"Yep, everyone's saying how hard you work taking care of Nora. Even Harold mentioned it to me. He said you'd taken over all the housework and cooking, besides helping the nurses day and night."

"Nanna's doing better, that's all that matters."

"You'll rest later, is that it?"

She felt her stomach tighten and begin to burn. "Nanna is all the family I have. Or at least it seems that way."

"What about your brother?"

"Oh, he's so busy making money in New York that he doesn't have two seconds of spare time. And either of my parents—" Her stomach felt on fire. "They wouldn't come here. When they heard about Nanna's fall, Mom offered to pay for a nursing home. A nursing home!"

Anger licked through her, and she knew it showed. "Nanna has always been there for me. She took me in when I was lost and alone that horrible year my parents were divorcing, and hers was the first real love I'd known. I can't leave her to fend for herself now."

"No, you wouldn't." The way he said it sounded like he believed in her.

And it comforted her like nothing else. That's what friends did, comforted one another. So why did she keep noticing the play of muscles beneath his T-shirt? Why was she feeling an electrical charge from being so close to him?

She *wasn't* attracted to him. She just *couldn't* be. She was off balance, that was all. Yes, that had to be it. She was out of her usual environment, like a fish out of water. That had to be why she was feeling this way.

The reason she'd let herself close enough to see Matthew's heart and feel her own respond.

"I catched a fish!" Kale's shout of delight shattered the definite tug of attraction between them. The boy hopped up and down, clutching the taut line of his play fishing pole. "Looky, Daddy! I got the big one!"

"Harold is always trying to catch the big one." Matthew winked as he tucked the oars into place and stood from the bench seat. Kneeling beside his son, with the other boys burrowing close to him, he reached over the gunwales and tugged on the heavy plastic line. An old leather boot popped out of the water, caught on the green plastic bobber.

"Sorry, son, but the big one fooled us again." Matthew kissed Kale's brow in comfort.

"Kale catched a shoe!" Ian giggled, and soon all three of them were laughing, the merry sound traveling across the gurgling river like birdsong, attracting smiles from a group of onshore fishermen.

"I bet Grampy Harold never caught a shoe before." Matthew winked at Hope as he wrestled the boot that was mysteriously tangled in the sturdy plastic line. "Hope, we're drifting toward that snag up there. See the way the water currents move around that spot in the river?"

"You mean the spot where we're heading?" She uncurled from the bottom of the boat.

"That's the one. Can you untangle this for me so I can steer the boat? I'd hate to capsize us on our first official date—you know that's what my mom's gonna call this. I'd never live down the embarrassment."

"Give me that pole." She towered over him with the wind in her hair and the sun haloing her with golden light. "I may be a city girl, but I know a thing or two about fishing. Move over, Kale, and I'll show you how it's done."

"You know how to catch fishes?" Josh asked, eyes shining. "Really, really?"

"Really. I went on a fishing expedition off Cabo San Lucas and saw big blue fishes the size of this boat."

"Did ya eat it?" Kale wanted to know. "Grampy Harold cooked the trouts we catched."

"No, I didn't want to kill anything so beautiful, but I got some great pictures of the sea." Hope twisted the boot, tugged on the waterlogged laces and the plastic bobber popped free. "Now, let's go fishing."

"Maybe you can catch the other boot," Matthew quipped as he guided the boat safely past the dangerous spot.

The way Hope laughed, easy and sweet, made him laugh, too. In fact, he'd drifted this river hundreds of times and he couldn't remember it ever being this beautiful or the day so bright.

Matthew hated pulling his truck into Nora's driveway and knowing the day was at an end. The sunset gathered in bold splashes of crimson, gold and purple along the jagged peaks of the Rockies, casting a lavender sheen over the peaceful land and regret through his heart.

"I'm going to call Patsy tonight," Hope said as she gathered her camera bag from the floor. "You've got three tired boys to deal with, so no arguments. Let me do it. I'll catch you at church tomorrow and let you know how it went."

"Matchmaking is harder work than I thought." They'd talked of nothing else on the drive back and had come up with an idea that just might work, or at least provide them some direction. "Fine, you talk to Mom. But I'm warning you, she's going to bombard you with questions about today. Nosy, probing questions. Be prepared."

"I'm brave, I can take it." Hope's hand moved toward the door handle.

"Wait right there, city girl. Sometimes you're too

fast for me. Just slow down.'' He hopped out, circled the truck and opened the door for her. ''Old habits.''

''Nice habits.'' She smiled and covered his palm with hers, although the independent flash in her eyes didn't fade.

Longing filled him, and he fought it. He stepped back an appropriate distance when he wanted to sweep her into his arms and nestle her against his chest.

Instead of being able to hold her and feel her sweetness, he had to be content with the springlike scent of her as she climbed down from the truck and released his hand.

It wasn't enough.

''I guess I'll see you in church tomorrow,'' she breathed, spinning around to face him, bathed in the soft lavender glow from the setting sun. ''Nanna insists she can make it, so I'm going to let her try.''

''I'll volunteer to carry her into the church and back out again, if she needs it. If she's not strong enough for the crutches.''

''That's a wonderful offer, thank you.'' She looked so independent, so beautiful. ''But strength isn't the issue. Nanna is plenty strong enough, and thank the heavens her pain is back under control. I just don't want her doing too much.''

''Let me know if you need anything, okay?'' He took a step back. He had to go. The boys were starting to yammer in the background, and the rising urge to reach out and kiss her was overwhelming him. He ached for her brightness, her sweetness, her sanctuary, and he had no right to feel this way.

No right at all.

''I told Nanna we're making a short day of it. Just

church and nothing else. So, at least we're safe from
another surprise brunch.''

''Don't count on it. There's still the Founder's
Days committee meeting coming up.''

''Yes, but Nanna will be staying home and your
mom won't be there, so how bad can it be?''

Famous last words, Matthew thought. It would be
tough sitting beside her through the hour-long meeting, smelling the shampoo in her hair and fighting an
impossible attraction to her.

''The day was the best I'd had in ages.'' Hope
retreated to the porch, sincerity dark in her gaze as
she looked at him one final time. ''I'll never forget
it.''

''Neither will I.''

Then she hopped up the stairs and, with the bang
of the screen door, disappeared from his sight.

But not from his heart.

''Have a good time with Matthew and his boys, did
you?'' Nanna asked from the kitchen table. A playful
glint sparkled in her eyes. ''Looks like you've got a
little sun. Or is that the first bloom of romance I see?''

''Definitely the sun, Nanna. Keep on dreaming, because marriage and I aren't happening.'' Hope
plopped her camera bag on the counter and snapped
open the refrigerator. ''Did you get some supper?''

''No, Roberta decided to starve me. Figured it was
the best treatment.''

''I can tell you're feeling better, you're starting to
get sassy.'' More happiness wedged into Hope's
heart. Yes, it had been a good day indeed. ''In the
mood for some iced tea?''

''Now there's a good suggestion. We'll sit down

right here and you can tell me all about your date with Matthew.''

Hope rolled her eyes. "It wasn't a date and you know it.''

"I know what I see.''

"Let's just agree to disagree on this, okay?'' She set the pitcher on the counter with a thunk. "It wasn't a date, I'm not looking for love, and poor Matthew is still grieving his wife.''

"Grief doesn't last forever. The loss does, but grief is like a wound.'' Her voice grew serious. "In time a heart does heal.''

"Oh, Nanna.'' Hope heard the truth in her grandmother's words. "I didn't mean to bring up something painful to you.''

"I'm strong, and I learned how to be a long time ago. The day I buried Jonathon was the saddest in my life, and the lowest point. The very lowest.'' Nanna stared hard at the table to hide the tears in her eyes, tears that never fell.

"I never told anyone this, not one soul, but I was furious with God. And I mean furious. He took more than my husband from me, He took my life, my reason for being.''

Hope took the chair closest to her grandmother and realized for the first time just how deep love between a man and woman could run, deeper than any river, higher than any mountain and stronger than death. "I can't imagine you being angry at God, Nanna.''

"I was hurting, honey, and let me tell you, the word 'rage' wouldn't have described it. I'd always seen Jonathon as the gift from God that he was, and the greatest light was our love together. And then one day Jon was so sick and soon gone. I'd shared most

of my life with him, and after twelve long years I'd
still give anything I have for one more day.

"Of course, I know I'll see him again. But it took
me a long time to accept His wisdom, to understand
that for everything there is a time. 'I trust in your
unfailing love. I will rejoice because you have rescued me. I will sing to the Lord because He has been
so good to me.'"

Hope didn't know what to say and didn't know if
she could speak for the tears knotted in her throat. So
she simply reached out and held her grandmother
tight and safe. But in her arms, Nanna no longer felt
fragile, but strong. She felt strong.

"We are so alike, Hope," Nanna said when she'd
pulled back to dash at the tears shimmering on her
lashes. "We both came from families where there was
no love, only war. Like you, I vowed I would never
marry. I'd never trust any man like that. I'd never live
with hard words and dark anger."

"I didn't know. I thought...." Hope looked around
at the old house where Nanna had raised her children,
where Hope's own mother had grown up in the bright
sunshine of Nanna's love, and not even that love had
protected Mom from a bad marriage. "I don't know
what I thought. That you came from a happy family."

"I fought falling in love, I can tell you that. But
God found me a patient man, one with fortitude and
a loving heart as infinite as eternity. I trusted in God's
love, and so I trusted in His gift of Jonathon's love."

"You found your happily ever after."

"Yes, I did. But Jonathon was on loan to me.
Every day is precious, and a day filled with love ever
more so. Please, don't waste your time stubbornly
protecting your heart, Hope. Life is far too short to

forsake God's gifts because we are afraid to accept them.''

Later that night, after tea, prayers and reading Nanna to sleep from her Bible, Hope felt the truth of her grandmother's words. Or maybe it was the contrast between the laughter-filled day and the unsettled aloneness of night.

She was glad Nanna had found love in her youth, one that had given her great joy, but Hope also knew the reason behind her grandmother's story. Nanna would not give up her stubborn desire to marry Hope off. Couldn't Nanna understand that Hope didn't need a husband? She had faith, she loved God, she tried to live her life the right way, but the memories of her and her fiancé's last fight echoed in the darkness surrounding her until her stomach burned and she flicked on as many lights as she could find.

Restless, Hope dug out her laptop computer and popped the small disk from inside her camera. As always, her work calmed her and centered her. She scanned some of the hundreds of images she'd taken on her interrupted trip to Italy, making notes of which ones she'd use for her next book.

Then she came across the pictures of the triplets she'd taken both in the garden and at the river. As she studied the images on her computer screen of three identically charming smiles and sparkling eyes, happiness slipped into her heart.

Nanna said that time was precious. Hope was glad she'd spent this day the Lord had given her with Matthew and his boys.

Chapter Nine

Matthew bolted awake, sitting straight up in bed in a room bathed in darkness, breathing hard. The wisps of dream remained before his eyes, the vision of Kathy at his side as they hiked through the mountains, her features blurring and her voice fading away into nothing, nothing at all.

The darkness felt choking and he kicked off the sheet, desperate to force the memory of the dream from his mind. But it wouldn't leave. The image of nothingness at his side remained.

Maybe he'd been unfaithful to her, to her memory. The vows he'd taken were until death do us part, but it was more than that. Love didn't stop with death, and he was at a loss what to do.

He tiptoed past the boys' room and found his way by memory and feel to the kitchen, where stardust and moonbeams silvered the bay window of the eating nook. A cold glass of water didn't dislodge the knot of emotion wedged in his throat or wash away the twisted-tight feeling in his stomach.

It's time. He heard those words like a voice surrounding him, more mysterious than the moonbeams slanting through the window. As he stepped into the silvery cast of the light, he felt the chasm in his heart tear open a little more.

He knew it was time to let go, to stop mourning. He couldn't bear to. For as long as he grieved Kathy, he still had a part of her. He was terrified that if he let go of his grieving then he would lose her completely.

His grief was all he had left of his beloved. And he felt guilty that he was ready to move on, ready to welcome sunshine on his face and feel again. And he was lonely. So very lonely.

Father, how can I do this to Kathy? Please, show me what is right.

His Bible was in the center of the table where he'd left it earlier in the evening, and he reached for it now, the smooth cover welcome against his fingertips, the weight in his hand an old comfort, the papery crisp flutter of the weightless pages soothing. The moonlight slanted over the type, and it was just enough to read by if he squinted.

''There is a time for everything, a season for every activity under heaven. A time to be born and a time to die.'' Matthew rubbed his thumb over the words, read so many times since Kathy's death. ''A time to cry and a time to laugh.''

He remembered talking on the phone with Hope the night of the last storm, and they'd laughed together. That wasn't the only time. On the picnic, Hope had made him laugh so many times that she'd chased away the sorrow in his heart.

The image of her, sun-kissed and gentle, flashed into his mind as she'd knelt with the boys in the boat.

Hope made him laugh. Made him feel. They'd run together through the field with the boys on their backs, racing each other through the sweet wild grasses, and he'd felt joy breeze over him like the wind.

"A time to grieve and a time to dance."

The moonlight slanted lower across the page, across words already committed to memory. Matthew closed his eyes, hating to admit it and knowing he could no longer deny it. For whatever reason God had brought Hope Ashton to town, the effects were felt in his heart. Her friendship had shown him exactly how alone he was.

As she'd fished with the boys, she'd illustrated unknowingly how much the triplets needed a woman in their lives, not a housekeeper but a mother. She'd shown him that the empty place at his side could be filled. Yesterday had been a gift, and Hope was a true reminder of what could be for him again.

In time.

Pain filled him, and it felt as if his heart were breaking all over again. But this time, unlike when he'd buried Kathy, there was no anguish. Now there was only peace.

After a long time, he opened his eyes and watched the moonbeams fade as the moon set. Soon the blackest point on the eastern horizon grew shadowed, then gray. Birdsong began like the most reverent of hymns—quietly, gently, building to a song of joy, of melody and harmony and hope.

Dawn broke softly over the Bridger Mountains, burnishing the snow-capped peaks with a rose-pink glow, and the stillness was shattered as three sets of bare feet pounded down the hallway. Three little boys wearing cartoon print pajamas bolted into sight, shouting good morning and racing to be the first to hug their daddy.

"Want waffles, Daddy," Josh asked as he fought his brothers to climb onto Matthew's lap. "Please, please?"

"Blueberry waffles," Ian specified.

"And lots of sausages," Kale added. "Please, please?"

Looking at the faces of his three boys, the truth struck Matthew like lightning out of a blue sky. He could never truly lose Kathy. She was here in their sons, in the shape of their smiles. And always would be.

Judging by the din of laughter and conversation spilling out of the open door of Manhattan's only specialty coffee shop, Hope figured she was late, at least by country time standards. It was still ten minutes to ten, but when she stepped through the threshold, she saw that hardly any chairs were available.

"Hope, you came." Helen pressed her hand in welcome. "How is Nora today? Did you let her up on her crutches yet?"

"She's doing better and no, not yet. She might be hopping around on them right now when I'm not there to watch her, but she'd better be off them when I come home."

"Atta girl." Approval beamed in Helen's smile. "You make Nora toe the line. She's far too strongwilled to listen to her doctors or her best friend.

Come, we saved a spot for you. This Founder's Days dance will be the best one yet.''

"I thought you were on the decorating committee," Hope began as she and Helen wove around the crowded tables.

"Yes, but you, Matthew and Harold might require a hand from time to time. A few of the committees overlap, like decorations. Believe me, you'll appreciate my help when it comes to making all those tissue paper flowers we'll need."

A waitress swept past with an empty tray, and suddenly Matthew was there, rising out of his chair, his smile easy and his gaze focused only on her. Even though he wore a work shirt and jeans, he looked exceptionally handsome and Hope felt as light as air as he offered her the chair beside his.

"I was saving this," he confessed. "With Harold in our group, our table has suddenly become very popular. I didn't want you to have to sit on the floor."

"You wouldn't have offered me your chair?"

"Not a chance." He waited until she was seated, then helped her scoot her chair in.

She couldn't remember the last time she'd experienced this courtesy. Not that she couldn't situate her own chair, but a cozy feeling wrapped around her as Matthew settled at her side, and with every breath she took she was aware of his presence.

"Look what I have for you." He pushed an index card across the table to her.

"Your fried chicken recipe."

"Remember, this is my secret formula. I'm trusting you with it."

"I'll guard it with my life. Wait, I have something for you, too." She reached into her handbag and presented him with a bound four-by-six book. "I couldn't resist. When you see them, you'll know why."

"What did you do?" He looked at her, his gaze speculative, his brow furrowed as he reached for the small photo album.

Hope watched as he focused on the first picture of the boys in Nanna's garden, contentedly playing with their trucks in the dirt. Their differences were evident in Ian's puckered brow, Kale's frown and Josh's sucked-in bottom lip. The boys were cute playing side by side, identical and yet distinct.

Matthew must have thought so, too, because when he looked up at her, his eyes shone with an emotion she didn't dare name. "I can't believe you did this."

"It was fun. Look at this one." She flicked the thick, plastic sheeted page to two more pictures, one on each side. "Look at the boys here. Running through the sprinkler. And here, when they noticed I was taking pictures."

"They started preening. Look at them." Matthew's gaze raked over the glossy photographs of his sons, first caught in action as they leaped into the sprinkler's spray and again as they posed for the camera, each showing his best smile.

"Keep turning. I took a lot at the picnic." Hope waited, buzzing with anticipation as Matthew flipped the pages, admiring the pictures of the boys running in the fields. She held her breath at the picture she loved of Matthew, with the wind ruffling his hair and Ian perched on his broad shoulders.

"I like this." Matthew tapped the image where three boys were caught in the act of devouring brownies, chocolate smudges and all.

"Look at them in the boat. This is my favorite." She leaned closer to turn the page. They were close. Maybe too close, but Hope couldn't force herself to move away. She turned the album toward Matthew so he could see the pictures of the boys, kneeling at the wooden gunwale and clutching bright green fishing poles.

"I don't know how you did it, but their personalities shine. You can see the differences in them at the same time you see they are exactly alike."

"I had to wait until they were unguarded." Hope didn't tell him that was the challenge of her work, finding the extraordinary in the ordinary, in color and light, in faces and landscapes. "Plus, the boys are good subjects. Kids don't come much cuter than this."

"I'm biased, so I gotta agree." Dark hazel sparkles lit his eyes, and she realized more intensely this time that they were too close, shoulder to shoulder, nearly chin to chin.

"You two are looking cozy," Harold commented as he pulled up a chair.

"Look what Hope did." Matthew turned the little book so that the older man could see the individual shots that Hope had taken of each boy.

Of Ian with fire in his eyes as he perched on his father's shoulder. Of Kale determined to catch the big one with his play fishing pole. Of Josh reaching with gentle wonder for a dragonfly as it hovered for one brief moment over the rippling waters of the Gallatin River.

"I hear those pictures you take go for thousands of dollars at fancy galleries." Harold shifted to get a better look at the photographs. "What would something like this cost a fellow like me?"

"How about a mocha with whipped cream?"

"It's a deal." Harold stood, heading for the front counter to order, and he was followed by three older women, all asking if he needed help on the dance committee.

Hope realized her arm was touching Matthew's, so she leaned back in her chair, breaking the contact. But the buzzing attraction she felt remained.

"Poor Harold. It's been like this ever since he moved back to town." Matthew flicked the book closed and ran his fingers across the blue flowered pattern. "Thank you for this. Kathy and I took a ton of pictures of the boys, but after the plane crash, I just stopped. Didn't have the heart for it, I guess. Or the time."

She could see there was more, but it was probably private and he paused, the appreciation lining his face unmistakable. "Thank you."

Hope nodded. She hadn't meant to make him remember his loss. "When I make prints for Harold, I'll copy off a set for Patsy, too. I should have thought to do it in the first place. My only excuse was that it was late at night and I was brain-dead."

"You're working at night?"

"Nanna's sleeping through the nights now. In fact, she's doing a lot better, but I'm going to be overprotective of her whether she likes it or not."

"I guess tomorrow night we'll test your overprotective skills." The sorrow in his eyes eased, and his smile returned.

Why did his smile scatter every thought in her brain? It took a moment, but she finally remembered what she was going to tell him. "When I talked to Patsy on the phone about inviting the Bible study group out to the house, she asked how our date went."

"What did you tell her?"

"I said we had a fabulous time, which was the truth. I'm getting fearless, here. Probably because I know the joke's on them."

"So, I take it you were able to invite more than Mom's Bible study group out to the house?"

"I thought we should celebrate Nanna's feeling better with an old-fashioned barbecue and potluck." Hope lowered her voice so it wouldn't carry across the table where Harold returned with coffee cups in hand. Helen took one side, and Mabel Clemmins took the other. "I even asked Harold to man the grill for me."

"How's Harold and Nora getting along?"

"Terrible." She leaned close to whisper and caught Matthew's man and soap fragrance. Awareness buzzed through her, and she fought to control the breathlessness of her voice. "Nanna won't look at the cabinet work until he's gone for the day, and she won't speak with him."

"How's he going to know if she's happy with his finishing work?"

"Good question. Twice he's come out to talk to her and both times she hardly looked at him. I hate to admit it, but so far we're dismal failures at matchmaking."

Matthew frowned, his gaze traveling across the small table to where Harold sat, seeming uncomfortable but unfailingly polite to Helen and Mabel. "She won't compete with her best friend for Harold, is that it?''

"Exactly." Hope looked sad. She thanked Harold for the coffee cup he pushed across the table. Lowering her voice, she leaned close enough to make Matthew's senses spin. "Nanna would never hurt her oldest friend. Maybe we'll have better success with your mom tomorrow."

"We'll just have to watch and see. I've interviewed a new housekeeper and she's going to take a trial run with the boys tomorrow night, so I can come help with the barbecue. If you want."

"I want. And that's great news. I hope she works out." Hope took a deep breath, but it didn't disperse the tangle of emotions tightening in her chest. She reached for her mocha and took a drink, letting the melting whipped cream and chocolate-flavored espresso roll over her tongue. But instead of soothing her, it only made her warm. Much too warm.

She leaned back, feeling flustered and embarrassed. What was wrong with her? Goodness, she *wasn't* attracted to Matthew. She wouldn't *let* herself be. Okay, he was handsome. About as handsome as a man could get. And he was nice, funny, kind and strong, dependable and more responsible than any man she'd ever known.

Not that it mattered. She wasn't going to forget the pain of her childhood and the fact that she'd almost repeated those patterns. The wall around her heart was in place. She was still safe, and Matthew's friendship wasn't going to threaten it.

It *had* to be Nanna's influence. Yep, that's what it was. Nanna's story of her husband and the love that still lived there had touched Hope's heart, that's all.

Made it seem like maybe, just maybe, true love could be possible for everyone. For her.

Okay, maybe that kind of love did exist, but it was rare. And the odds of finding it had to be astronomical.

No, a person couldn't go around hoping a fairy tale would happen to her. Hope turned her chair as Helen stood and called the room to order and the last of the waitresses hurried to serve the coffee and tea.

She'd been alone all her life and wanted to keep it that way. At least if she stayed single, there would be no husband's angry words and no insults hurled like sharpened arrows.

Relying on love had been the worst mistake of her life.

She'd never make that mistake again.

Matthew couldn't take his gaze off Hope. She wore a white dress that draped her gently and brought out her rose and cream complexion. Wisps of her hair danced in the cross breezes from the open windows and doors.

"I'll handle contacting the band," Helen offered. "Last year's country players had such a great time, they wanted to come back. I don't think we'll have a problem getting them."

"Thanks, Helen." Hope jotted something down in a small notebook she had open on the table before her, and thick locks of her hair tumbled over her shoulder to flutter against his forearm, soft as silk.

She riveted her gaze on Harold. "You'll make sure the community hall is still reserved?"

"I'll make sure of it." The older man nodded.

"Great." Hope turned. The smile touching her lips

looked rose-petal soft. The impact of her gaze was like a touch to his soul. "Matthew, do you have anything to add?"

"N-no," he stammered, a little embarrassed that he was staring at her beautiful mouth. "I guess this means we're done. Until next week."

Their small meeting broke up, although the coffee shop was loud with the laughter and good-natured arguments of other committees trying to nail down the details for the big event.

Hope looped her purse over her shoulder. "Are you off to another job?"

"Not until this afternoon." He waited, gesturing for her to pass, then followed her around the edge of a table toward the door. "How about you? Do you have to get back home to Nora?"

"Eventually. I'm hosting the barbecue and potluck tonight, remember?"

"I remember." He reached over her head and gave the screen door a shove before she could catch hold of the handle. "How about you and I grabbing lunch together?"

"I'd like that since I'm absolutely starving."

"Starving, huh? Can you make it across the street to the diner?"

"If I can find the energy."

"Here, you'd better take my arm."

She looped her arm lightly through his, and they fell in stride as they hopped down the stairs and across the street. There were only a few cars to dodge. Too soon he was holding open the door for her and she breezed past him, her dress whispering around her, and led him to a booth in the back where geraniums were blooming in a pot on the windowsill.

Matthew snagged the menus from behind the salt and pepper shakers and handed one to Hope. "People are staring at us. Maybe this wasn't such a good idea."

"I'd forgotten this about small towns. Everybody probably knows what Patsy and Nanna are up to."

"And they think it's working."

"That's right." Her gaze met his full force. "We've become friends, and I'm glad."

"Me, too." Friends. Matthew skimmed the menu, feeling her gaze on him, feeling...just feeling. The loneliness in his life remained, but being with Hope made him happy. Friendship was more than he expected from this woman different from him in fundamental ways. "If you're back to work, does that mean you'll be leaving soon?"

"I have a book I'm supposed to be starting, but I'll have to put it off until Nanna's able to take care of herself." She looked wistful, as if she missed her work, but the love for her grandmother shone unmistakably. "I just wish my mom showed some interest in her welfare."

"Besides suggesting a nursing home?"

"Exactly." Hope nodded, her throat working, her gaze troubled. "My brother offered to take care of Nanna, but Noah's in New York, and she didn't want to leave her home. At least he calls every week. Mom, well, it's hard to believe she came from here."

The waitress arrived, an old friend from high school, and so the ordering took longer with the exchange of hellos and news. Jodi Drake lifted one brow at him, the question clear in her eyes. *What is a woman like her doing with you?*

Matthew shrugged. It was a good question, but this

was no date. It was two friends having lunch. Jodi returned with two sodas in tall glasses and finally left them in peace.

Of course the entire café had quieted, as if the people he'd grown up with and gone to school with, and whose houses he repaired, were straining to listen in on their conversation.

Hope's eyes laughed as she tore the paper from the end of the straw. "I'm resisting the terrible temptation to say something really scintillating, not that I could actually do it."

"You mean, like starting a rumor? That could be dangerous. We're probably already engaged according to the gossip that's out there."

"I said it was tempting, not that I'd do it." Hope took a sip of cola, eyes sparkling with laughter.

Their food arrived, and he told himself to put a stop to his budding feelings for her. Hope Ashton might be out of his league, but she was his friend. And for that he gave thanks as he bowed his head in prayer.

Across the table he heard Hope's gentle amen, and he wondered if she felt this, too—this feeling of harmony, as if the angels smiled down on their friendship.

"I never answered your question," she began as she spread the paper napkin across her lap. "Since I'm stuck here in Montana—"

"Stuck?"

"Okay, happily visiting Montana, I won't be able to fly back to Italy to work, but I figured I might be able to work here. I got some great pictures the day you and your boys let me tag along."

"You really did enjoy the trip downriver, didn't you?" He liked the way she lit up at his words.

"I loved it. Montana's beauty is spectacular, and I think I can get some work done while I'm here."

"You happen to be in luck." Matthew grabbed the ketchup bottle from the end of the table. "I happen to know my way around this countryside."

"Oh, boy." She stole the ketchup bottle from him. "I suppose this means you're volunteering to be my tour guide?"

"Yeah, I guess it does." Friends. That's what they were.

But that wasn't a satisfying thought. Not at all.

Chapter Ten

"I take it your lunch date with Matthew went well?" Nanna asked, eyes sparkling. "Because he's speeding that truck of his down my driveway. Probably in a rush to see your lovely face."

"Ha! He's bringing over his barbecue like a good *friend*." Hope slipped an aqua barrette into place in Nanna's gray hair. "I'm not even going to ask how you know Matthew and I had lunch together. A *friendly* lunch, nothing more."

"How did I know?" Nanna's chuckle was as merry as lark song. "It wasn't noon yet, and my phone started ringing. Notice how it's been ringing all afternoon?"

"It often rings all afternoon. You have a lot of friends, Nanna." And maybe one male friend would change her life. Hope took solace in that thought as she clipped the matching barrette into place.

Nanna had found true love once. She certainly could find it again. "You look beautiful."

"I would look better if you'd let me back up on my crutches."

"There's no chance of that. You'll overdo it, I know you. It's only a few more days until we head back to the orthopedist. If he says the bone is still mending to his satisfaction, I'll take your crutches out of hiding."

"You're awfully bossy for a young woman. Does Matthew know about this? Maybe he won't discover it until after the wedding."

"Sure, go ahead and tease. I can't imagine where I get my bossiness from."

"From your father's side of the family, surely."

"Certainly not from you." Hope laughed as she held the small silver hand mirror for her grandmother. "What do you think?"

"You work magic on me, that's for sure." Nanna peered around the mirror to see out the bedroom window as Matthew parked his truck alongside Harold's and called in greeting to someone at the back of the house. "Who all is coming to supper tonight?"

"You'll just have to wait and see. Now, if you'd agree to let me put your bed downstairs, we wouldn't have to negotiate those stairs."

"This is only temporary, young lady. By this time next week I should be in a walking cast, so hide my crutches all you want." Merriment sparkled in Nanna's eyes as she scooted off the edge of the bed and straightened, standing on one leg.

"You fall down now and you can say goodbye to that walking cast." Hope shook her head and retrieved the light aluminum crutches from the corner of the room. "How about I find a handsome man to help you down the stairs?"

"That Matthew is terribly handsome, isn't he? Makes a woman turn her head twice and wonder if he's a good kisser."

"*Nanna.*" Hope nearly stumbled over her own feet, and the crutches slipped from her fingers. The crutches clanged as they clattered to the floor, and she bent to retrieve the awkward things. "You are incorrigible, you know that?"

"I know."

"You look far too pleased with yourself. Well, fantasize all you want. You'll eventually see how wrong you are." Hope held the crutches upright in front of her grandmother. "Now, careful. I don't want you falling."

"'You can make many plans, but the Lord's purpose will prevail.'"

"What is that supposed to mean? You're the one matchmaking, not God." Hope fit one crutch under Nanna's arm. "And no, don't try to tell me it's part of His plan for me. I'm independent, I'm happy and I don't mind staying single. It's better than the alternative, believe me."

"But Hope—"

"No, not another word." Hope helped Nanna with the second crutch. "And don't tell me about Grandfather again, okay? I know you found happiness, and I'm glad. I believe there can be happiness in some marriages, I do. Just not for me."

She nearly tried the alternative, and what did it get her? Heading toward the same kind of misery that her parents lived through. She'd made the right decision and broken off the engagement, but she wasn't going to spend her life wishing for the kind of rare, impossible love.

She wasn't about to believe that true love would happen to her.

A floorboard creaked behind her, and she spun around to see Matthew outside the open door, a sheepish look on his face. "I came up to ask where you wanted the grill, Hope. Nora, you look breathtaking."

"And you are a shameless charmer." Nanna took a wobbly step. "Now, help me down the stairs, young man, and tell me, do you plan on flirting with my granddaughter over supper?"

"I was thinking of flirting with her *after* supper." Matthew winked at Hope over Nanna's head.

"You aren't helping, Matthew," Hope warned.

"I do think there could be some flirting." He tossed the words back as he took Nanna's elbow and held her steady as she hobbled into the hallway.

"And you, Matthew Sheridan." Nanna's step was wobbly but her voice rang as strong as ever. "Those boys of yours need a good woman to mother them. And a woman doesn't come any better than my granddaughter. Maybe you've noticed that by now, if you're as smart as I think you are."

"I noticed that right away, Nora." Matthew's gaze found Hope's and held it. She could see so much on his face, in his eyes, in his heart. Strength. Kindness. Humor. A goodness that ran soul deep.

Hope's step was shaky as she led the way down the stairs, keeping a few steps ahead of Nanna in case she needed assistance. But she didn't, and after the older woman was settled on the garden bench in sight of the grill Harold was setting up, Hope pulled Matthew aside in the kitchen.

" 'The wicked are trapped by their own words,' "

she reminded him. "You deliberately misled her and now she's going to have our wedding planned before she's off those crutches."

"She'll be too busy with her own to worry about us, you wait and see. I'll be right about all the flirting that will be going on, it just won't be between us." A saucy grin tugged at the corners of his mouth. "Anything is possible."

"I'm not going to argue about that."

"Are you two lovebirds done flirting in there?" Nanna called from the garden, her voice drifting through the open window. "Do you need a chaperone?"

Hope felt embarrassment creep up her neck and heat her face.

Matthew splayed one hand on the counter and gazed through the ruffled curtains. "Nora, behave."

Laughter rose on the wind, and Hope realized Nanna wasn't alone. Good grief. Who was out there listening to them? She squeezed next to Matthew and peered across the budding roses, clematis and hollyhock to the bench where Nanna sat, surrounded by half the senior citizens from church. Patsy was seated beside her, and the two of them were beaming.

"We're in trouble now." Matthew laughed as he looped his arm around her shoulders, and Hope didn't step away. Cozy warmth seeped into her, and for the first time since she could remember, she felt safe. Completely safe.

Boy, it was a good thing they were just friends. Because if they weren't, she might really fall for Matthew. And what good could come of that?

While Matthew and Harold cooked beef patties and hot dogs on the grill, Hope made sure gray-haired but dapper Joseph Drummond was on Nanna's left and polite Claude Winkler on her right. Helen was one of the women helping with the food, and Hope noticed her at the grill, holding a platter steady for Harold to fill with hamburger patties.

But Harold wasn't responding to Helen's gentle flirting. He was merely being polite. After Helen left with a look of longing on her face, carrying the platter to the table crammed with potluck dishes, Hope caught Harold's quick glance across the lawn to where Nanna sat, making conversation with two men.

So, Harold *did* like Nanna—a lot. Hope plopped a scoop of Patsy's baked beans onto the sturdy paper plate she carried and watched Harold turn away. He looked troubled and filled with regret. Mabel scurried up to him with adoration in her eyes, and the distinguished man merely smiled politely as he checked the thick German sausages that Matthew was turning to see if any were done.

And because Nanna didn't want to hurt Helen, she wouldn't acknowledge Harold, much less act on their mutual interest. Hope's heart sank as she squirted a thick ring of mustard on the top half of a fresh hamburger bun. It didn't take a genius to realize that both Jake Drummond and Claude Winkler liked Nanna, especially Claude. A retired rancher and a new widower, Claude had a genuine smile and the tough wiry look of a man who'd earned his way in the world. Jake Drummond was all gentleman as he took Nanna's paper cup to refill it from the pitcher of iced tea in the middle of the table.

Hope finished the garnishes on Nanna's hamburger and carried the full paper plate across the lawn. She wanted her grandmother to be happy. She wanted her to find a love to brighten the rest of her days. With Harold?

Nanna looked happier than Hope had ever seen her, with color high in her cheeks and her eyes twinkling like stars. "You, my dear, are a fine granddaughter. Surprising me by bringing all my dear friends here."

"Now you know why Matthew and I were conspiring. To figure out a way for you to attend Bible study without going very far on that leg."

"You can't fool me, young lady, but I won't press you tonight. No, tonight we will have fun, fellowship and take time to remember our Lord." Nanna pressed a kiss to Hope's cheek. "Now, go on, have some fun. See if you can get Matthew to take a break from the grill."

Hope shook her head at her incorrigible grandmother and left her in good company. The din of happy conversation and the rise and fall of laughter lifted on the sweet evening breezes. The mouthwatering aroma of sizzling hamburgers scented the backyard as Hope grabbed a paper plate for herself.

Matthew stepped behind her, and the memory of his cozy warmth lashed through her. "Leaving Harold to handle the grill?"

"Yeah, he told me to eat, then we'll switch. He doesn't look in a hurry to sit down and let the single ladies fawn over him. Notice how he keeps glancing in Nora's direction and not in Helen's?"

"I noticed." Hope added a handful of carrot and celery sticks to her plate. "And Helen keeps watching Harold. Let's face it, we're doomed as matchmakers."

"Nora seems to be getting a lot of attention from Jake and Claude."

"Yeah, but she doesn't have that look in her eye. The one that Harold puts there. Or used to before Nanna realized Helen was serious about Harold." Hope grabbed the salad tongs. "We're not faring any better with your mom."

"I've been watching her all night. She hasn't shown any interest in any of three single men her age." Matthew heaped a helping of pasta salad onto his plate. "Want some?"

"Sure." Hope stepped close to his side and it was a nice place to be. "Have you noticed your mom avoiding anyone?"

"What?" As if considering the question, his brow furrowed and his eyes narrowed, and he scanned the crowd scattered around the half dozen picnic tables. "Well, yeah. Dr. Corey. She's got her back to him. I noticed him behind her in the food line earlier, but she didn't talk to him."

"And your mom talks with everyone. Is she always like this with him?"

"Beats me. I know she goes to his son for medical treatment, but not Andrew."

"Right, for her allergies." Hope wrestled a hot dog bun from a plastic bag and dropped it on her plate. "Isn't that weird, that she'd see someone our age instead of a man she'd gone to school with? A man with more medical experience?"

Matthew nodded slowly, his gaze pinning Hope's as bold as a touch. "I'm going to look into it. You're not half bad to have around in a pinch."

"I've been known to be useful now and then." But she heard the deeper meaning behind his words, and her heart twisted hard enough to make her catch her breath. Matthew liked her. And that knowledge made her feel good. Very good.

Too good. The caring bright light in his eyes was one of the most beautiful things she'd ever seen, and for no reason at all, she felt that after a lifetime of battling uncertain seas, lost and alone, she'd found her safe harbor. She longed for him to wrap her in his arms and pull her against his iron-strong chest.

For this one moment the loneliness vanished, replaced by the sweetest tenderness she'd ever known or felt from another human being.

And he was someone she could never call her own.

"So what's the holdup?" Mira McKaslin asked from behind them.

Embarrassed at herself and laughing, too, Hope tucked away those wishful thoughts, no, *foolish* thoughts, and reached for the potato salad spoon.

As twilight deepened in thick shadows, Hope retreated to the kitchen to fetch the box of citronella candles and tried not to watch Matthew as he worked with several men to push the picnic tables together to form one big square. But it was impossible to look at the bunch and stretch of his muscles beneath the cotton shirt he wore and not ache to be held by him.

A warm wind gusted through the window, bathing her with the sweet scents of wild grasses, roses and moonflowers, and she remembered what she'd come to the kitchen for in the first place. She grabbed a book of matches from the top drawer by the steaming coffeemaker and was turning around when the air in the room changed. It became electrified, and then Matthew was striding through the threshold, his dark hair tousled by the ever-present wind and his big hands loosely fisted at his sides.

Aching, just aching, Hope took one step back, knowing with the lights on in the kitchen that anybody in the yard who was looking could see them clearly. Not that she was in danger of reaching out to Matthew. Wanting and reaching were two separate things.

"I pulled Harold to the side of the house to wash off the grills and asked him what was going on with Helen. She seemed awfully interested in him." Matthew joined her at the counter and took the matchbook from her. "He assured me he's done nothing to lead her on. The day they went to church together, they'd accidentally met in the parking lot and since she had no family with her that day, he didn't want to leave her alone."

"He's a gentleman." Hope tore at the shrink-wrapped box, trying to act unaffected. "Let me guess. He felt obligated to invite Helen to brunch that day."

"Exactly. He told me that he'd explained to her that he wanted to be friends."

"Did you ask how he felt about Nanna?" Hope wrestled open the box and began setting candles on the counter.

"We didn't get that far. Mabel came up and interrupted us so she could flirt with Harold." Dimples flashed in his cheeks as Matthew lit a match. "Ever since he's moved back to town, he's been a real popular fellow. But have no fear, I promise I'll try to get the truth out of him. Nora's cabinets are nearly finished, so we're running out of opportunity."

"Did you find out anything about your mom and

Dr. Corey?'' Hope set the last candle on the counter and stepped back so Matthew could light it.

''The night's still young.'' Matthew blew out the match and tossed it into the sink. ''It's strange thinking of finding love for my mom. She's been without Dad for a long time.''

''Having second thoughts?''

''No way. I want her to be happy. And I'm trying to look at it this way, a guy's never too old to get a new stepdad.'' His gaze dropped to her mouth.

Hope shivered. Heat spilled through her veins, and she didn't know what to say.

Together they carried the lit candles out to the tables where the party was calming down and Bibles were appearing out of handbags. Men and women settled on the benches as Hope carried out pitchers of iced tea and a thermos of decaffeinated coffee.

''What a wonderful surprise.'' Nanna caught her hand when Hope handed her a paper cup filled with brisk iced tea. ''I've so missed Bible study.''

As Hope kissed her grandmother's cheek, love warmed her heart. Love for this rare woman of substance and joy, of gentleness and affection. Hope didn't know where she'd be without Nanna's love, and she was grateful for it. Nanna was her family—God had truly blessed her with a beautiful grandmother.

''Hope, I saved you a place,'' Patsy called out as the group quieted. ''Right here between me and Matthew.''

Hope tried not to blush as she circled around to the far table. Matthew stood, shrugging one wide shoulder, the apology already in his eyes.

''I tried to stop her,'' he whispered, his breath hot

against the shell of her ear. "But she just wouldn't listen to reason. This matchmaking thing has gone to her head and affected her judgment. I'm considering looking into medication."

"Some nice antipsychotic drugs, you mean?"

"Exactly." His hand cupped her elbow as she swung her legs over the bench. His touch was like midsummer, and all too soon he'd pulled away.

But the memory of the touch remained.

His mom led the way across the darkness of Nora's driveway, the rhythm of their steps sounding loud in the peaceful night. "Wasn't that just the best time?"

"A real thrill," Matthew said.

"Now, don't go being sarcastic with me. I know you had a good time. I *saw* longing in your eyes for Hope Ashton."

"What you saw is none of your business." He opened the car door for his mother.

"Admit it. You're finally over Kathy and ready to move on with your life."

He winced and nearly dropped the casserole dish his mom handed to him. Kathy wasn't someone he would ever be able to erase from his life and forget. "I'm not looking for a replacement for Kathy. I'm not going to forget her and what she was to me."

"But she's in your past, dear." Mom sighed. "I didn't mean to hurt you, but Matthew, look at what's in front of you and not behind. Can you try to do that for your mother, who loves you more than anything?"

"Sure, use guilt and manipulation to get what you want." He kissed her cheek, the familiar scent of White Diamonds perfume and baby shampoo reminding him of a lifetime of her good-humored affection. "I'll follow you home to make sure you get there safe."

"A son who dotes on his mother. I'm glad to know I raised you right." She brushed her hand along his jaw. "Now indulge me in finding me a daughter-in-law. Not a replacement, but an addition. Someone for me to shop for. Someone to force to go to lunch with me and who'll raise my grandsons right."

"I see where this is heading." Matthew slipped the dish on the floor behind the driver's seat and stepped back so his mom could climb behind the wheel.

He would follow her home, make sure she got in all right so that she wouldn't face a dark, empty house alone.

As if he could feel Hope's gaze, he turned around and gazed up at the white, green-gabled farmhouse, but the lit windows were curtained. Maybe it was wishful thinking, or maybe it was because he wanted to hold her in his arms.

"Matthew's a wonderful man, isn't he?" Nanna asked as she eased onto the edge of the couch. "I doubt there's a kinder man running around loose in this town."

"I don't know about that. Harold seems like an awfully nice man. Don't you think?"

"Sure, but he's not for me, little one." Nanna's smile faded. "I could sure use a cup of chamomile tea."

"I can take a hint." Hope grabbed the crutches and leaned them against the wall, walking past the spot where Matthew had almost kissed her. Uncertainty balled hard in her chest. "I'm not going to badger you the way you badger me, but consider this. You've got a lot of years ahead of you still, and wouldn't it be nice to have someone to share your future with?''

''I can ask you to consider the same.''

Laughing, shaking her head, Hope crossed the room and headed toward the bright lights of the kitchen. She saw a flash of movement and heard a rustling sound in the corner, but before she could become alarmed, Harold strolled into sight wrestling with a garbage bag.

''A raccoon found its way in while the last of the crowd was leaving,'' he explained with a simple shrug and the steady, kind gaze of an honest, good man. ''He was probably attracted by the smell of food. I scooted him on out of here and thought I'd make sure all the garbage was tight in the can before I left. Don't want you girls having any troubles tonight.''

Hope bit her lip to keep from chuckling. She wasn't afraid of a raccoon, but Harold's thoughtfulness was a kind gesture, and she didn't want him to think that she didn't appreciate it. ''You and Matthew did a fantastic job cooking tonight. I'd never had corn cooked on a barbecue before.''

''Imagine that. You had to travel the world over to find good corn on the cob.''

''They do a lot of things right here in Montana.''

''That they do.'' Harold finished knotting the big white plastic bag. ''I'll just take this out. Got to do one more thing and then I'm out of your way.''

Hope watched him leave, a man still tall and strong, unbowed by the years. Anyone could see he had a good and genuine heart. If only there was a way to bring Harold and Nanna together. Two lonely people deserved love, and there was no mistaking the longing in Harold's gaze whenever he looked at Nanna.

After she put tea water on to boil, she punched the playback button on the answering machine. The tape screeched and clicked, then began to play. Her brother's voice, as deep and nearly as overbearing as her father's, apologized for missing them. Hope glanced at the clock. It would be after midnight in New York, but Noah would be up. She punched his number and waited. Sure enough, he answered the phone on the second ring.

"You should be in bed sleeping," Hope told him.

He laughed. "Now don't start on me. You know I'm a night owl. How's Nanna?"

As they talked, the tight uncertainty in her chest began to ease. Her big brother always had been able to make everything right—well, as right as anything could be in their family. And he hadn't shed the scars of their childhood, either.

Hope feared those wounds would never heal. For the time it took the water to boil and the tea to steep, they talked of his work and hers, of Nanna's progress and of her and Matthew's matchmaking scheme. She had him laughing by the time she asked if he wanted to talk with Nanna.

Carrying the phone into the living room, she wasn't paying attention until it was too late. Harold was with Nanna. He must have come in the front door. He was offering a bouquet of flowers to the stunned-looking woman on the couch.

Hope took one silent step back before they noticed her. She hid in the shadows, afraid to retreat farther because of the squeaky floorboards. Could this be it? Was Harold going to start courting Nanna?

"I'm sorry, Harold." Nanna lifted her hand to refuse the beautiful bouquet. "I don't like cut flowers. Maybe there's another woman who'd appreciate them."

Harold mumbled an apology, obviously hurt, and tried to make pleasant small talk as he retreated toward the front door. Hope's jaw dropped, and she couldn't believe her ears. Sympathy for him welled within as he tossed one last look of longing toward Nanna, then quietly left the house.

"I'm not interested in him, so don't look at me like that."

Hope didn't argue. She didn't know what to say. This matchmaking scheme of hers and Matthew's wasn't turning out like she'd planned. Pain darkened Nanna's eyes and made them bright as if with tears.

"Noah's on the phone. He says he's looking for a gorgeous woman to talk to."

"That flatterer." Nanna took the receiver, the pain lingering even as the pleasure of speaking to her only grandson lit her smile. "Noah, you ought to start flirting with women your own age and then maybe you'll find one who'll marry you."

Hope retreated from the room to check on the tea. It had steeped long enough, and the earthy freshness of chamomile steamed when she lifted the ceramic lid. She loaded the sugar bowl and creamer on a tray and found one of Nanna's favorite china cups in the dining room hutch. She carried the tray upstairs, the faint sound of Nanna's voice keeping her company as she wandered down the lonely hall to the room at the end.

She set the tray on the corner of the nightstand and walked to the window. Since she hadn't bothered to turn on the lights, the room was as dark. With the lacy curtains fluttering around her, she gazed out on the night. Bright stars twinkled in a velvet sky so black it glowed.

Unlike in the cities, here it was dark enough to see the smaller, dimmer stars that winked from so far away, stars nearer to the edge of heaven. The pink haze of the Milky Way swirled across a piece of the night with no moon to dim its amazing radiance.

And lower, she could see the faint cut of headlights illuminating the landscape where the end of Nanna's long driveway met the county road. A car followed by a pickup slipped out of sight as the road lifted and dipped. It was Matthew's truck. She knew it. It had to be. Aside from Harold, he and Patsy had been the last to leave.

What was she doing? Aching for the chance to be held safe and warm in Matthew's arms?

Please, Father, show me what to do.

But there was no answer as the night seemed to darken and the chirping of one raccoon calling another sounded from the fields. The echoes of the happy evening and of Matthew's warmth remained, and not even the night breezes could disperse them. There was nothing she could do to erase the longing to be in his arms—his strong, safe arms.

Or the way her blood felt strange, tingly warm in her veins. Why was she feeling this way? It was more than friendship she felt for Matthew. Much more.

Love could hurt. It could tear a person apart. It could take a whole heart and reduce it to dust. She trusted God to keep her safe from it, and He had. He'd kept her from marrying Christopher. He'd reminded her that to some He gave the gift of singleness.

And that meant Matthew was no threat to her heart. Her feelings for him were just a reflection of her wishful thinking, of the little girl inside her still looking for love.

That was all. Hope was sure of it.

The night was silent, and she felt small and alone. So very alone.

Chapter Eleven

"Harold told me what happened." The sound of Matthew's step echoed against the bare walls and high rafters of the community hall. "He crashed and burned."

"Nanna actually lied and said she didn't like cut flowers, like the entire house isn't filled with them." Gladness radiated through her at the sight of Matthew, dressed in denims and a royal blue T-shirt. "Harold came this morning to finish polishing the cabinets and attach new handles. I brought Nanna out to see, and she wouldn't look at him."

"Wasn't she happy with his work?"

"The cabinets are beautiful and they match the new linoleum so nicely. She told him so, but in this distant voice that's so unlike her. I know she likes him very much, but when he went to say goodbye, he'd brought her another gift. A beautiful rosebush. She turned it down."

"How did Harold take it?"

"He just nodded, grabbed his toolbox and left. She's doing this because of Helen."

"Then that woman's a bigger fool than I gave her credit for." Helen tapped across the polished wood floor on her low-heeled pink sandals, her spring dress fluttering with her rapid movements. "I know what you two are up to. I overheard Patsy and Nora chattering on about their success with you two, and it doesn't take a fool to figure out why half of the unmarried population over fifty was in Nora's backyard."

Hope couldn't tell if Helen was angry with her, too. "I wasn't trying to force Harold and Nanna together. I know you like him, and so I made sure Nanna had plenty of handsome men to talk with at the table."

"I saw." Helen's eyes sparkled even though her mouth was pinched. "And I saw how Harold kept looking at Nora. Over and over again. Now, don't get me wrong. I'd grab hold of that man in a second, but only if he wants *me* to grab him. And what about you, Matthew? Trying to marry your mother off, too?"

"If I can."

"Well, that explains the time you're spending together, doesn't it? You're letting everyone think you two are an item to keep those two matchmakers from matchmaking again. I see what you're up to. Marry them off instead, and they won't mind so much that you were only fooling them."

"It sounds awful when you say it like that." Hope looked to Matthew for help, but he only shrugged. "We're not being deceitful. Matthew and I are only friends, and I've told Nanna that over and over again."

"Just be careful, dears." Helen clucked, shaking her head and changing the subject. "Now, since I'm in charge of the Founder's Days decorations, I get to meddle in every subcommittee. Let me tell you, the balloons and tissue paper flowers we had in here last year were stunning."

Hope fell in stride beside Helen who tapped merrily around the hall, making suggestions that would tie the theme of the celebration together. Over the top of Helen's carefully hair-sprayed curls, Hope caught Matthew's puzzled gaze. He seemed to be asking, what have we gotten ourselves into? Hope shook her head, completely at a loss.

After they'd surveyed the hall, Helen hurried off, digging in her big purse for the car keys to her beloved Ford Falcon. "One word of advice for you, Matthew. Consider this. Your mother planned to go to the senior prom with Dr. Corey. I know because my Jenny is the same age and they were friends. There was a terrible falling out. Have you noticed how Patsy drove all the way to Bozeman to see a doctor until Andrew's son joined the practice?"

Matthew shook his head. "I don't see how she's going to marry a guy she won't even talk to."

"I didn't say she wouldn't marry him." Helen winked as she turned over the engine. "You two *friends* be careful."

"You're an angel, Helen." Hope waved as the Ford Falcon crept out of the parking lot and inched toward the empty street. Helen honked, stuck her hand out the open window to wave and inched down the street with great care.

Hope turned to the man towering beside her, casting her in his shadow. "How did your boys like the new baby-sitter?"

"Good enough so that I hired her. Millie's easy-going and gentle and nothing seems to faze her, so I think she'll work out. Least, I hope so." A slow smile tugged at the corner of his mouth—his very handsome mouth. "I hear from my mom that Nora is up on her feet with a walking cast, which has got to mean she's healing."

"It does. She's not getting around a whole lot because there's still quite a bit of pain, but that shouldn't last for much longer."

"So, is she feeling well enough for you to spend the afternoon with me? I promised you some sight-seeing, and I mean to deliver on that promise."

"You want to show me that you're a man of your word, is that it?"

"Sure, or my reputation will suffer. Is that a yes?" He strolled into the shade made by her Jeep and his truck, parked side by side. A tow truck slowed to a near stop on the street behind them. The driver gaped at them through the open window.

He waved and Matthew waved, then the truck sped off with a roar. Matthew shook his head, chuckling. "My reputation is going to suffer when you leave town. Everyone is going to shake their heads and say, that Matthew Sheridan, don't know what he was thinking of, but he didn't have a chance with that beautiful Ashton woman."

"No, they'll be saying, what's wrong with the woman because she won't grab hold of a man like that." Referring to Helen, who'd said the same about Harold, she made Matthew laugh. "She gave us a good clue about your mom. What are we going to do next?''

"Try to put them together, I guess.'' Matthew shrugged. "Not that it worked so well with Harold and Nora.''

"Putting them together isn't going to work unless they'll talk to each other. Maybe what you should do next is ask your mom why she won't speak to Dr. Corey.''

"I wanted to avoid that, because she'll tell me to mind my own business.'' Matthew winked. "But I'm not afraid of my own mother. She's a secretive sort, but I'll uncover the truth. Don't you worry. My sanity depends on it.''

A car passed on the street, slowing down for a good look. Then it zipped off, and Hope thought she recognized one of the waitresses from the café.

"See what I mean?'' Matthew crooked one brow, his humor as warm as the sun above.

Hope liked this man far too much. "I need to stop by Nanna's to change and grab my camera before you can steal me away.''

"Now, if my mother heard you say that, think what ideas that would give her.''

Laughing, Hope tugged open the Jeep's door. Although she fought, it was strange how places in her heart felt alive whenever she was around Matthew.

Matthew squinted against the harsh sun and shouldered open the door to Harold's stable. "How long has it been since you've been on a horse?''

"When I'm home, there's a stable I ride at.''

"Then you own your own horse?'' He followed her inside the dim warmth where light sheened against wood and off the straw-strewn floors. Where the scents of sweet hay and horse lingered in the air.

A wistful look tugged at Hope's features as she nodded. "I miss her when I travel. She's a good friend and a great mount. I learned to ride during the year I stayed with Nanna. She kept cattle on the land, and I rode her mare out to check on them."

"I remember." The neighbors rented the vast pastures that comprised most of Nora's land, Matthew knew. "I thought you might like seeing Montana on horseback."

"You thought right." Hope breezed past the empty stalls. "Where's the tack room?"

"At the end of the row on your left." Matthew grabbed the saddlebags Harold kept just inside the front door, ready to go and packed with essentials like antivenin for snakebites, binoculars and a first aid kit. Slinging the bags over his shoulder, he caught up with Hope, who was in the tack room hefting a saddle onto her shoulder.

"Grab the other one, will you?" She tossed him a sassy grin with a hint of challenge in it. That city girl sure liked to do things for herself.

Well, he wasn't going to argue with her. This time. He tossed two blankets over his forearm and grabbed Firebrand's saddle. The small room felt smaller as she breezed past him so close that they almost touched.

Then she was gone, tapping away in those fancy leather boots, looking like a million dollars in worn Levi's and a turquoise shirt. Her luxurious hair was tied back in a ponytail, which swung in a gentle rhythm with her gait.

His skin burned, and he felt the need to hold her, to take her in his arms and tuck her against his chest.

He hurt with wanting to hold her, and it took all his willpower to let her walk away.

He heard her steps hesitate. The jingling sounds told him she'd snagged the bridles from their hooks just inside the corral door.

The two horses had already come to investigate. Friendly, they stood side by side and nosed Hope's hand. Then, when they weren't satisfied, they started bumping against her.

"Hey, you two," she scolded lightly, adjusting her balance due to the heavy saddle she carried.

Matthew scooped a handful of sugar cubes from the box on the shelf, then loped down the aisle into the corral. "This is what they're looking for. Harold always hides treats in his pockets, which is fine until a guy comes along unknowingly and gets accosted by these greedy brutes."

Firebrand whinnied a welcome and shook his head, his platinum mane sweeping along his golden neck. Spying the treats, he neatly scooped four cubes off Matthew's palm. "Watch out, they're spoiled gluttons."

"Yeah, and vicious, too." Hope laughed as the more polite of the two Arabians lipped her hand in a persistent, gentle request. "Matthew, give me some of those sugar cubes if you know what's good for you."

"Or what, you'll feed me to Firebrand?" He dropped a half dozen cubes onto her palm. Those hands—why did they keep attracting his attention? Everything about her did, the way her smile lit her eyes, the dark silken wisps that framed her face, how she laughed. All he could think of was the way she touched the world—with gentle, loving hands.

And a gentle, loving heart.

He noticed she'd looped the bridles over the end post of the corral, and that gave her one free hand to deal with Morning Glory. The horse managed to get a couple of cubes before Hope slipped the rest into her jeans pocket.

"Now, stand still and be good." She tipped the saddle onto its side and stole a blanket from him. "Harold must do a fair amount of riding."

"He's an true outdoorsman. Now that he's moved back to his family homestead, he heads out on horseback into the wilderness to fish and camp. Sometimes, if Mom's feeling brave enough to take care of the boys for a few days on end, Harold and I head out together."

Hope smoothed every last wrinkle from the blanket she'd tossed over Morning Glory's withers. Matthew did the same on Firebrand, and the horses stood patiently, eager for a run. Matthew's heart squeezed when he watched Hope lift the saddle as if she'd done it every day of her life, and then tighten the cinch. Morning Glory settled down once Hope tugged the chestnut forward a few steps and pulled the cinch in a notch.

Matthew finished saddling Firebrand and tied the saddlebags into place. "Let me know if you need help with Morning Glory. You're going to need gloves and a hat. You might as well use Harold's. I'll fetch 'em for you."

"Thanks." She exchanged the mare's halter for the bridle with quick efficiency, then dug a sugar cube out of her pocket.

Matthew's fingers faltered on the buckle, and he

could only stare at the woman who seemed to be able to do anything—even make his heart feel again.

Here in the sunshine, the loneliness ebbed away until he felt only the heat of the sun on his back and the longing for Hope in his arms.

"I'll be right back." He left the reins trailing to the ground and Firebrand nickering with a demand for more sugar and retreated to the stable's dim interior.

Matthew knew he was feeling this way for a reason—it was time to move on, time to start living again. That was all. It couldn't be more, even if he wanted it to be.

He found Harold's hat and gloves and stepped into the sunshine where she stood watching and waiting for him.

"It's going to be a little big," he warned as he dropped the black Stetson on her head. "But it will keep your nose from burning."

"Hey, I'm not picky. I'm just glad to be here." Hope took the gloves and slipped them over her slender hands one at a time. Delight shimmered in her eyes, and she made him feel far too much.

"Need a boost up?" he asked, even though she was already reaching for the saddle horn.

"Not a chance, cowboy." With easy grace, she eased into the saddle and tightened the reins as Morning Glory sidestepped.

"That's a girl," Hope praised when the mare calmed, and she patted her hand, lost in Harold's glove, against the horse's velvet neck.

She straightened in the saddle like the seasoned rider he'd figured she was, and he mounted Firebrand.

The gelding pranced, scenting the wind, eager for the chance to stretch his strong legs.

Hope's appreciative gaze scanned the Arabian he rode and then higher. Matthew felt a spark of realization zing through him—he wasn't the only one affected by their closeness. But before he could think that through, Morning Glory broke into a trot toward the heavy wooden gate at the end of the corral. Dust rose in the horse's wake, and Matthew didn't have to urge Firebrand into a trot.

"Sure, show off your riding skills." His voice might be teasing, but he couldn't deny the flicker of warm pride in his chest as Hope opened the gate, backing the Arabian with skill. Morning Glory tried to balk, but Hope soothed her with firm assurance. The Arabian gave up the fight and obediently stood.

"After you." He sidled Firebrand alongside her. "I thought you might like to ride into the foothills. We can keep to the river if you want, but something tells me—"

"I want to get closer to those mountains." The Bridger Mountains shone like polished amethysts, the rugged range of snowcapped peaks so close they filled the entire eastern horizon. Hope shone, too, and he couldn't look away.

Sweet native grasses and wildflowers in vivid purples, yellows and oranges rustled in the warm winds. The sun burned warm on his back as Firebrand tugged at the bit. Matthew knuckled back his Stetson so he could get a good look at the woman at his side.

He saw the challenge in her eye and the toss of her head as she pushed the too-large hat out of her eyes. And in a flash, he knew what she was thinking, saw her grip loosen as she gave the mare more rein. Hope leaned forward in the saddle.

At the same moment he gave Firebrand his head, and the gelding stretched out with his long legs. Shoulder to shoulder the horses ran, and only wind and air separated Matthew from Hope. He couldn't tear his gaze away from her, so different as her ponytail came loose and her ebony locks danced and rippled in the wind. His heart felt alive, like a dark place touched by a new sun.

Happiness like spring bloomed inside him, and he laughed as he gave Firebrand his head and the gelding broke into a full-out gallop, shooting in front of Hope and Morning Glory. He laughed at the surprise on Hope's face and then he was in the lead, leaning into Firebrand's windswept mane and feeling the horse's amazing power as he flew across the earth.

The wind in his ears and the drum of Firebrand's hooves kept him from hearing Hope's approach, but when he glanced over his shoulder, there she was, leaning low over Glory's neck and whispering quietly to her. The mare's ears were flattened, her nostrils flaring as she chewed up the ground, drawing closer. Anyone could see the challenging tilt to Hope's chin.

Matthew could feel his pulse pound in his ears as Firebrand reached the fence marking the pasture's northeastern boundary. Breathing hard, he spun the Arabian around to watch her ride in. She was grace and fire and it made the happiness inside his heart burn hot as the sun above.

She reined in, at ease in the saddle. Her hair was wind-tossed and Harold's hat had fallen down her back, dangling by the string that had caught around her neck. ''You had a head start, or we would have beaten you. And I'll prove it to you on the way back.''

''Is that a dare?''

''Count on it.'' She sparkled, and she made him sparkle, too.

''Is that an eagle or a hawk?'' Hope leaned back in her saddle to squint at the perfect blue sky. A great bird the color of brown sugar lowered her wings as if she were stroking the wind, then soared over the rise of a hill.

''Looks like a golden eagle to me.'' Matthew pulled a pair of binoculars from the saddlebags and handed them to her. ''Here she comes again.''

The brush of his fingers on hers made her feel safe somehow, as if no harm could come to her. She lifted the binoculars with one hand and searched the sky for the majestic raptor, aware of the world around her. The wind sang through the needles of the lodgepole pines and the Douglas firs lining the trail. Pine grass crunched beneath the horses' steeled hooves, and saddle leather creaked as she shifted her weight.

''Right there.'' Matthew's words tickled against her ear as he nudged her wrist toward the east.

The snowcapped peaks stood in high relief, and she searched the sheen of glaciers until she spotted a blur of golden-brown. The eagle soared closer until she seemed near enough to touch. Hope watched breathless as the great bird nosed into a swift dive, swooping toward the grassy earth, talons hooked and outstretched. In one smooth motion the eagle brushed the ground and in an arc soared straight into the sun.

Inspiration struck, and Hope shoved the binoculars in Matthew's direction and snatched the small camera buttoned in her shirt pocket. In the space of a breath she caught the eagle on film, flying on the shafts of the sun, light gleaming on copper wings.

"See where she's heading?" Matthew asked from behind his binoculars. "Look at the cliffs above the river. She's got a nest there. She must have new babies because she's keeping close to home."

Morning Glory was stretching her neck to lip at some of the sweet grasses in the shade of a boulder. Hope switched the lightweight Nikon to her left hand and leaned over the saddle horn to snare the fallen reins.

They rode with the sun at their backs and the wind in their faces in companionable silence. It was enough that she was with him.

"Look down there." Matthew halted Firebrand at the rise of the hill, where the rugged earth plunged downward into a steep river canyon. The waters of a silent river winked in the sunlight below where five or six dark objects were wading into the current.

It was too far away to take a good picture without a different camera, but she could make out the thick, wide bodies covered with brown-black wool and the humped back and shoulders of the creatures as they crept ever deeper into the cool mountain-fed waters.

"It's like something out of the old west." She lowered her camera and slipped it into her shirt pocket, then buttoned it in tight. "They must be wild."

"Yep. There's a buffalo range for them that backs up to the national park. Now admit it, this isn't something you'd see on those worldwide travels of yours."

"I freely admit it." Wonder shone in her eyes as she dismounted with one graceful movement. "I can't believe in all this time I've never been back. Nanna loves to travel, and so it's easier to fly her to where I am. But to come here…I guess I've avoided it.''

"Too small-town for you, is that it?"

"No." She led Morning Glory to the very edge of the rise and she stood alone facing the majesty of mountains and sky. "Nanna's house was the first real home I'd known when I was a girl. I came here with a world of hurt inside me, and to tell you the truth, it's almost like coming back to that place in my life. Not exactly. I'm different, life is different, but it makes me remember."

"And it's coming home."

"Yes." She said the word on a sigh, quietly, and it touched him like nothing else.

Matthew had always known the security of a home, the nurturing love of his parents and then of his wife. Even with the grief and loneliness of missing Kathy, he'd never been truly alone. He'd had God's assurance, his mother's love and friends he could count on.

He dismounted, the saddle creaking in the vast peace of the hillside, and joined Hope on the edge of the precipice where only wind filled the enormous canyon. "With Nora up and walking, I suppose you'll be leaving soon."

"Afraid I'll be leaving you to coordinate the Founder's Days dance single-handed?"

"Sure. I guess I have the right to know if you're going to dash off to Europe and leave me holding the bag, or if you'll stick by me just in case things get tricky."

"Do I look irresponsible?"

No, but she didn't belong here. She might look at home with the wind teasing her ebony locks, dressed in a casual shirt and jeans, but she had no reason to stay, not when the entire world stretched out before her like a big red carpet.

"Now that you mention it, you *do* look irresponsible," he teased, because there was no way to say what was in his heart. "Everyone here knows you can't trust someone from a big city."

That made her smile, a brightness of her being that lured him closer. Like a rainbow at the end of a storm, like the first brush of dawn's light after a dark night, and he longed to hold her, just hold her.

"I've got Nanna to marry off, remember? And your mom. Which reminds me." She flicked a lock of dark hair behind her ear, a simple gesture, but one that left him riveted. "Since we're at such a dead end with Nanna, we've got to concentrate on your mom. It's too bad there isn't a way we can get her and Andrew together."

"Already tried that. She ignored him."

"Okay, we have proof. We're total and complete failures as matchmakers." Hope sat on the ground and crossed her legs. "Maybe this means I'm doomed to endure Nanna's advice for the rest of my life."

"So, I take it this means you never plan on marrying?"

"What's wrong with that?"

"Nothing." Matthew eased down beside her. "Even a big-city girl has to have an admirer here and there."

"Being from the city is a big flaw, is that it?"

"Sure. At least around here." He liked watching her laugh, light and sweet, liked the way her beauty shone from within. "You must have wanted to find someone."

"I did once." She stared down the canyon wall at the Gallatin River threading through the lush green valley below, and she looked lost. Her easy confidence faded and her voice saddened. "I thought that just because I'd come from a painful family, it didn't mean I was stuck with those patterns. That I could break them and find the home and family I'd always longed for."

"You fell in love?"

She nodded once, and he watched the muscles in her jaw tighten. "His name was Christopher and I thought he was so wonderful. I really thought——" She paused, looking hard at the buffalo so very far below. "I thought he was everything my father wasn't. Gentle, encouraging, loving and kind. We dated for three years, because I had to be sure. Absolutely sure before I agreed to marry him."

"But you didn't marry him."

"No." Her shoulders slumped perceptively. "After we were engaged, he started changing. I don't know, maybe it was me. Maybe I made the ultimate mistake of thinking I could make a marriage work, that love could last. But when I let my guard down and trusted him, he changed. He tried to limit what work I did and started checking up on me when I traveled. I was working as a photographer for an ad agency and living with my brother in New York at the time. I was working very hard at my job, and Christopher became possessive. He didn't want me to work."

"I know a lot of men feel that way because they want to be good providers," Matthew said evenly. "But this was about control, wasn't it?"

Hope nodded. "I tried to talk to him about it, and he became so angry. It was like he'd been hiding this other side of his personality, and I recognized my father in him. I knew if I married Christopher, then I would be sentenced to a life like my mother's. She married Dad for his money, and I wasn't going to make a similar mistake of marrying someone because I needed to be loved. It would have ended the same.''

"I'm sorry that happened to you." Matthew could see her sorrow and something larger and deeper, and it saddened him. "Believe it or not, there are men in this world who aren't like that. A few outstanding, handsome individuals a woman can trust."

"Like you, is that it?"

He laughed. "Are you saying I'm not?"

"It's certainly debatable." But her heart ached with what could never be. "I took Christopher as a sign that I was better off forsaking my dreams of happily ever after."

"Or maybe it was a sign not to marry that particular man."

"With my past, maybe marriage isn't an option. I know that's what God was telling me." She tried not to let the words hurt. "I must have gotten the bad marriage gene that runs in my family."

"There's a gene for that?"

"Sure. Apparently there's a recessive gene on Nanna's side and a great big dominant one on Dad's. He comes from a big wealthy family and everyone's been divorced at least twice, I think."

"Now see, we have more sense than that in Montana." He winked so she knew he was kidding, and his gentle humor was like the sun's touch to her heart.

"The light is changing. Wait, I want to get a picture." She had to move away from the comfort of being by his side. He felt suddenly too close, and she'd revealed far too much of herself.

Dark-bottomed thunderheads gathered in the sky behind them, threatening to cover the sun. Shafts of light textured the background of turbulent clouds, bright against dark. If she climbed on that boulder, she'd get the right angle.

"Do you always work when you're supposed to be having fun?" Matthew asked, saucy.

"This *is* fun." She crawled onto the huge rock, powdery dirt clinging to her knees and hands as she scaled to the top. *Perfect.* She framed the shot. "I'm having a rip-roaring time."

When she turned the camera on him, he lifted one hand. "No, you don't. I'm getting camera shy."

"Too bad." She captured his slow easy smile and the wind ruffling his hair before slipping the camera into her pocket. "It's getting late. I bet you have to get home to relieve your baby-sitter."

"Right you are." Matthew gave his horse a sugar cube from the palm of his hand. "I'm looking forward to our race. Firebrand and I intend to win, just so you know. And the winner gets…"

"A meal cooked by the loser?" Hope offered as she climbed from the rock.

"It's a deal."

The instant her boots touched the ground, she heard the chilling clatter of a snake's distinctive rattle. Right next to her ankle.

Chapter Twelve

❧

Fear struck her like lightning, leaving her weak and terrified.

"Don't move. Not an inch." The quiet strength in Matthew's calm voice penetrated her panic. "That rattle is his warning. He won't strike first, not as long as you back away nice and slow."

"Are you s-sure about that?"

"Positive. He's probably more scared of you than you are of him."

"I don't know. I'm pretty scared. And his mouth is open. I can see his fangs." The snake, curled up in the sun, hadn't awakened from his nap in the best of moods, and his V-shaped head swiveled toward her as if taking accurate aim.

"Just back up like I told you," Matthew's voice soothed. "Slowly."

She heard a snap as he tore a dying limb from a spindly fir and stalked toward the boulder, out of the rattler's sight. "I don't think I can move."

"Standing there is making him nervous. Come on, just lift your right foot. Trust me, Hope."

"Okay." Every instinct she had screamed at her to run, but she took a deep breath. *Please, help me, Lord.* She shifted the weight off her front foot and eased back a single step.

The snake didn't strike. Coiled tight, tail rattling, he watched her with cold eyes, front fangs glistening.

"That's it, another step, Hope." Matthew's voice rang with calm assurance.

She managed another step away and still the snake didn't strike. Shaking, she spun and flew at Matthew. Before she knew what she was doing, her arms were around his neck and she was safe against his strong, wide chest. The fast beat of his heart beneath her ear told her he'd been just as afraid. Her feet lost touch with the ground as he lifted her to a safe distance from the rattling snake.

"You're okay, Hope." His hand curled around the back of her neck, his fingers winding through her long hair. "He didn't get you."

"He startled me. I should have been watching where I was going." Her words were muffled because her face was pressed into his shirt. *Thank you, Lord.*

"Next time we'll do a rattlesnake check before we let you start climbing around with your camera."

"Good idea."

She felt like heaven in his arms, like forever and a day, and he wanted to tip her chin up and kiss her gently until her fear vanished. But kissing her wasn't a good idea. Not a good idea at all.

She broke away, thanking him for rescuing her, and he caught Morning Glory's reins for her because she was shaking badly.

He wanted her in his arms again, but the moment for that had passed. Visibly shaken, she mounted and took the reins from him. The brush of her hand on his lit a warmth inside his heart. A warmth that didn't fade as they headed to Harold's land, racing toward the barn with Morning Glory nosing Firebrand out of a win.

The warmth in his heart lingered far into the evening, when the lonely hours stretched before him like an endless sea. All he could think about was her smile, her brightness, her grace. All he wanted was to hold her in his arms again.

The ringing phone snapped Hope's concentration from her computer screen to the clock above the stove. It was nearly midnight, and she grabbed the receiver before it could ring again.

"Hope?" Matthew's cello-rich voice rumbled across the line. "Is it too late to call? I figured you'd be up working."

"You're starting to figure me out. That can't be good." Hope rubbed her tired eyes, exhausted from staring at the computer screen for hours on end. She'd been working because it was better than remembering the exciting, protective shelter of Matthew's arms. "I'm taking a look at the images I took today. I'm really happy with a couple of them."

"The eagle and the thunderheads?"

"Among others."

Hope tapped her mouse, and the image on the screen changed from the golden eagle soaring to heaven on a sunbeam to the image of Matthew's half smile and twinkling eyes. The light burnished his strong shoulders and highlighted his wind-tossed hair.

In a single frame she could see the laughter in his eyes and the character in the man.

She grabbed the glass of soda on the table next to her computer and leaned back in her chair. "Are you calling with plans for the meal you owe me?"

"I have to show you that I'm not a sore looser. The only question I have is do you want to eat with or without the boys. I mean, it's hard to enjoy a quiet meal when they need refereeing."

"I've been brushing up on my refereeing skills."

"Then you'll have a chance to put them to use." His voice so far away felt like a touch, comforting and welcome. "How does Saturday sound? After the planning committee meeting?"

"It's a date. How are the boys doing with the new sitter?"

"So far so good. Josh takes a while to get used to change, but he's doing better. All three have been asking to see you. They want to go fishing with you again. They even told it to my mom, and boy, did that make her smile."

"I bet it did. Is she hearing wedding bells?"

"Imaginary ones. Her hold on reality is slipping. It's a shame. I wonder if this happens to all grand-mothers?"

"It looks that way to me. When you dropped me off, Nanna had to hear all about our date, as she called it. I told her you had romantically raced me on horse-back through a field and I nearly stepped on a rattler. Just your typical dinner and romance kind of date."

He chuckled, a mellow, attractive sound that touched her deep inside. She couldn't remember ever laughing with a man like this, maybe not even in her entire life. He made all her worries fade until she felt as light as air.

"Oh, I have news on the matchmaking front, but not good news." Hope stood up and paced to the window, the cordless phone propped between her ear and her shoulder. "Apparently Helen and Nanna had a heart-to-heart today about Harold. Helen told Nanna to go for it."

"What did Nora say?"

"That it wouldn't be right to set her cap for Harold now. She won't compete with her best friend, even after all this."

"That woman is stubborn, but principled. I can't imagine who she reminds me of."

Hope laughed. "Go ahead and charm me. It's not going to ease the sting of failure."

"At least we haven't messed up the Founder's Days dance so far."

"Not yet. There's plenty of opportunity left."

"What does that mean? That you're counting on failing?"

He laughed and although miles separated them, she felt as if he were with her. "I've got Millie to promise she'll baby-sit for me that night. That means there won't be three little boys at our knees tripping us when we dance."

"You're actually going to dance with me? In public?"

"It's a rough job, but someone's got to do it. Besides, five of my buddies have called wanting to know if I've snared the most eligible woman in Gallatin County."

"The most elusive, you mean. I had a great time

today. I mean, a *really* great time. Thank you, Matthew."

"Any time."

She heard in his voice that he'd enjoyed their afternoon, too, and so she hung up the phone with a smile. No man had ever made her feel like this. No man had ever made her feel as if there was really such a thing as romance, really such a thing as a man's honest love.

"When's Hope comin', Daddy?"

Matthew felt a tug on his jeans and looked down to see Joshua gripping a dump truck in his free hand. "She should be here soon. We'll have to wait until she gets here."

"Why?" Innocent hazel eyes gazed up at him.

At about a thousand whys a day, times three, Matthew merely rolled his eyes and tried to ignore it. "Go out and play with your brothers."

"They wanna know when Hope's comin', too."

"Tell them to be patient." Matthew passed a plate beneath the faucet and plunked it into the bottom rack of the dishwasher.

"Then can we have more cookies?"

"You boys just had some. Outside and get some fresh air." Matthew wiped his hand on a nearby towel and reached down to ruffle his youngest son's hair.

"Why?"

Finally Josh was convinced enough to head outside, leaving a trail of sand in his wake on the clean floor. Watching them through the window, Matthew finished up the past-due breakfast plates. By the time he turned off the faucet there were more tracks of sand across the kitchen.

"Is Hope coming *now?*" Ian asked, rubbing a clump of sand out of his hair.

"Right now?" Kale seconded.

"Now, Daddy? Now?"

"You boys are impossible." But Matthew wanted to see Hope, too. All it took was one trip down the river for the triplets to like her. And Matthew figured it had taken him even less time. He'd liked her the moment he'd spotted her broken-down Jeep alongside the road that stormy night. Every time he saw her, he liked her more.

"So, is she comin'?" Ian rubbed more sand out of his tousled hair. "She squirted us with the hose, and we gots a sprinkler."

"Yeah, Daddy, we gots a sprinkler." Kale and Josh spoke nearly in unison, their identical faces upturned with the widest, sweetest pleading looks on the entire planet.

Okay, so maybe he wanted to see Hope, too. "Go outside and play and she'll be here before you know it."

Three little boys opened their mouths to protest and were cut short by the chime of the doorbell. Cries of "Yippee!" and "Hope! Hope!" preceded him to the front of the house. His heart was beating fast with anticipation as he reached for the brass knob. But it was Mom standing on the front step, arms full of plastic containers.

Matthew swallowed his disappointment. "You didn't have to bring vats of food."

"Well, Nora and Hope make two extra to feed, and if Harold shows up to grill his specialty burgers, I swear he can eat a big bowl of potato salad all by himself."

Matthew lifted the heaviest containers from the collection in his mom's arms and held the door for her as the triplets shouted, "Gramma! Gramma came, too!" and threw their arms around her knees, holding tight.

Matthew managed to speak above them. "Harold isn't coming. He found out that Nora would be here and bowed out."

"That's a shame. Doesn't that woman know he's carrying a torch for her?" Patsy blew kisses at her grandsons and agreed to their pleas to see the big hole they dug in the sandbox. "Helen told me what you two kids were up to, trying to play matchmaker for Harold and Nora. I think it's sweet, but you need a professional's touch, dear."

"A professional like you?" He shut the door with his foot and followed his mother and the trail of sand left by his sons down the hallway to the kitchen. "You were so successful with Hope and me. We're planning a June wedding."

"You are?" His mom turned, a brief second of joy on her face, then she shook her head, scowling. "I can't believe a son of mine would tease me like that. Your brothers have better manners, but you, Matthew Joseph, are the scoundrel of the bunch. I actually believed you."

"How does a dose of your own medicine taste?" He set the containers on the counter next to the refrigerator. "Come on, Mom. There's no way Hope Ashton is going to marry me, so stop dreaming."

"Who's dreaming? Anyone can take one look at that girl and see she needs a family." She thunked several containers onto the counter and told the boys, yes, she would be right there. "Hope Ashton looks lost and alone, and besides Nora, what true family does she have? She's got a good heart. Anyone who would take the time to care for her grandmother is certainly good enough to marry my son and raise my grandsons.''

"Sure, but next time you matchmake, try to find me someone a little more realistic, okay?" He opened the refrigerator and started stacking the containers inside.

"What's this, you aren't scolding me for trying to marry you off? Can it be that God has answered my prayers?"

"Don't go dancing a jig or anything, but if I fall in love again, I'll remarry. Sometime in the far future." He smiled as his mom wrapped her arms around his middle and hugged him fiercely.

"Now don't make me wait too long for more grandchildren. I love my triplets, but Matthew, they are growing up and pretty soon I won't be able to bribe hugs and kisses out of them." She stepped back as the doorbell rang again. "Well, not unless I use my car as a bribe. I bet that's Hope."

"Hope!" "It's Hope!" The cries rang through the air as the boys pounded from the kitchen and raced down the hall.

"Son, let me sweep up after them while you greet your *girlfriend*." His mom waggled her brows.

Matthew swung the refrigerator door shut and shook his head. "I'm going to talk to the pastor about you. I think you need some serious counseling."

She laughed, shooing him away with the broom she'd snatched from the corner.

The boys had already flung open the door to reveal Nora with Hope standing in the bright threshold.

Hope had a wicker basket slung over her forearm, and her hand was on Nora's elbow.

Matthew's heart stopped beating when Hope turned her attention from the doting, noisy triplets and greeted him with a smile. A genuine smile from her gentle heart, and everything inside him—all his hopes, his dreams, his needs—remembered holding her in his arms. He craved the feel of her sweet and warm against his chest and the peace that came with it. A deep, abiding peace.

"I brought Nanna's special secret baked barbecue beans." Hope lifted the basket just enough to emphasize it. "And baked cinnamon rolls."

"Yippee!" The shout filled the air. "Cinnamon rolls!"

"I know how to be popular with the three-year-old set." She laughed when Ian took hold of her basket.

"I carry it, Hope!"

"That's my job." Matthew lifted the heavy basket from Hope's arm and breathed in her scent. Memories of their day on the mountainside assailed him, and the peaceful feeling in his heart doubled. He knew he shouldn't feel this way, but he couldn't help it. "Boys, out of Nora's way. Nora, it's been a long time since two such beautiful ladies have graced this house."

"You big charmer, you." Nora wasn't fooled as she took the arm he offered. "No wonder my granddaughter has fallen for you."

"Nanna, you're impossible. You see, Matthew, Nanna has this lovebug theory. That eventually everyone is going to get bitten."

"And here I forgot to put on my flea collar this

morning," he quipped. "Knew I'd forgotten something."

"I remembered mine, so never fear." Hope winked at him. "Can the lovebug bite a person at any age?"

"That's what I've heard," Matthew answered.

"You two!" Nora huffed, amusement glittering in her eyes as she took a careful step on her walking cast. "I'm going to go out into the yard with Patsy and sit a spell. We have a world of visiting to catch up on."

"As long as you two beautiful women aren't plotting our wedding, I'll allow it." He said it just to make Hope laugh again.

After sending the boys outside to play and escorting Nora to the comfortable shaded chairs beneath the old maple trees in the backyard, he realized he'd lost Hope. He found her kneeling in the grass next to the sandbox, intently listening while the boys talked in triplicate, demonstrating with their trucks.

He had a perfect view of them through the kitchen window above the sink—a perfect view of her. Dressed in tan pleated shorts and a melon tank top, she looked like the girl next door and not a woman of means. When the boys started throwing sand and a spray hit her in the arm, she merely laughed and gently admonished them. Then she helped Kale brush sand from his face.

Something inside Matthew changed as he watched Hope with his sons. Her touch was as caring as any mother's, her words as gentle, her manner as nurturing. He could hear the melody of her voice through the open window, carried by the warm breezes. Kale thanked her and, with a child's open heart, threw his arms around her and hugged her tight. Hope hugged him back, sand and all, and a smile touched her face as Ian and Josh hugged her, too.

His heart ached with an emotion he dared not name, because he *couldn't* be falling for Hope. He wouldn't let himself. *Lord, please don't let me feel this way,* he prayed, but his feelings remained, growing stronger with every breath as Hope kicked off her sneakers and climbed into the sandbox, claiming a bulldozer as her own.

Hope felt the touch of Matthew's gaze as she played trucks with the boys and through the entire time she spent running around his backyard with the hose, squirting the giggling triplets with cold water. On the sidelines, Nanna laughed and worked at her knitting, her needles clicking along as she chatted with Patsy.

After the boys were thoroughly drenched and shivering, she turned off the hose. "Time to dry off, boys."

"But we're firemen!" Ian argued, grabbing the nozzle for himself.

Hope stopped him before he could turn it on and blast his brothers with it. "Firemen also have to dry off and get ready for lunch. They all eat together at the firehouse."

"Hamburgers?" Kale asked skeptically.

"Lots of hamburgers." Laughing, Hope looked up and nearly dropped the hose she was coiling as Matthew stalked across the lawn toward her.

The muscles in his legs rippled beneath sunbronzed skin and other muscles worked beneath his navy-blue T-shirt as he tossed a towel to each boy. "The coals are on hold. I put cinnamon rolls on the picnic table, one for each of you. Sit down and use your manners.''

"Cinnamon rolls!" The triplets raced, towels fluttering behind them like capes, their voices lifting on the warm breezes. "No, Josh. Don't sit there." "That one's mine." "Don't push." Then they turned quiet as they started eating.

"Food works every time." Matthew leaned close, so close she could see the smooth shaven texture of his jaw and the green-brown flecks in his hazel eyes. "The boys had a blast. Thanks for taking time with them."

"My pleasure. Can I have that last towel you're holding?"

"On one condition. Go horseback riding with me again."

"What about the boys?"

Matthew's grin dimpled as he pressed the beige terry towel into her hands. "Mom can watch them. We'll tell her we want to spend time alone."

"Are you sure that's wise?"

"Mom deserves what she gets. Look at her, gloating over there with Nora. Guess what I did?"

Hope bent to swipe the towel down her lower legs. "I'm afraid to ask."

"Invited Dr. Corey over for lunch. He just called— he had an emergency he had to deal with but he's on his way here. He lives next door." Mischief flashed in his hazel eyes. "He was outside watering his rhododendrons when I stepped outside to fetch the morning paper, and I couldn't resist."

"Leave it in the Lord's hands, you said." Laughing, Hope stood on one foot to dry off her toes. "Your mother doesn't know, does she?"

"Do you think she'd be looking so happy and relaxed if she did?" Matthew caught hold of her wrist, and his touch brought back the memory of being held by him, of sunshine and laughter and the safe protection of his arms.

She yearned for that security again, to feel the thump of his heart against her cheek and his muscled strength. Even though she knew it was a dream she could never believe in.

"Sit right here," he whispered, and she gasped in surprise to find a bench directly behind her. When she sat, Matthew knelt in front of her.

He cupped her right foot at the heel and rubbed the towel across her arch with slow care, then over the ball of her foot and down the length of her toes, leaving a tingling trail. Hope felt the tension ease from every muscle she owned, and she leaned back against the wooden bench with a sigh.

A doorbell rang in the distance. "Hey, Mom, would you get that for me?"

"You're terrible," Hope laughed as Patsy set down her crochet work and hurried into the house. "What if she scares him away?"

"I don't think so. Funny thing, when I told Dr. Corey that my mother would be here, he agreed to come." Matthew dragged the towel over the top of Hope's foot, finishing with slow caresses.

Her breath caught sideways when Matthew's warm, callused fingers caught her other foot and began a wonderful, luxurious massage that left her unable to think. She felt as if she were floating on clouds and sighed again.

"There. Let me grab your shoes." He reached for her canvas slip-ons and eased them onto her feet. This man who'd spent the last few years of his life caring for his sons now took care of her.

No one had ever pampered her so much. Hope felt lost when Matthew stood and offered her his hand to help her from the bench. She placed her palm to his, and his fingers curled around the side of her hand. At his touch, fire shot through her veins and tenderness welled in her soul. Her feet touched the ground and she suddenly stood breathless in front of him.

They were so close, their breaths mingled. So close she could see his pupils dilate and his bottom lip quiver. His hand skated in a slow caress up her wrist and forearm to band around her elbow. For one second the world, the boys' shouts, the wind in the trees, Nanna's cheerful welcome to Dr. Corey, faded away until all Hope could feel was the tight, tingly plummet of her stomach to her knees. Her mouth quivered with anticipation as Matthew's lips hovered closer, a fraction above her own, waiting, just waiting.

"Matthew!" Patsy's shrill voice rang through the air from very far away. "Matthew Joseph Sheridan, I want a word with you. Oh…my. Not right now."

Matthew groaned, winced and moved away. Over his shoulder she could see Patsy just inside the back door, hands to her face, horror-struck that she'd interrupted.

"I'd better go calm Mom down," he said, apology rough in his voice. His gaze slid once more time to her mouth and then he moved away, leaving her wanting, leaving her wishing for a fairy tale she wouldn't believe in. A fairy tale that could never come true.

"One more time, Hope. One more time." Ian, secure in his jammies, leaned back against her and tipped his head up to stare at her with big innocent pleading eyes, exhaustion bruising the delicate skin. "Please, please."

"Please, Hope." Josh snuggled against her side, warm and sweet, smelling like shampoo and little-boy goodness. Kale on the other side hugged her as he yawned, just as dear.

"You boys know I'm a total softy, but this is the last time."

Yawns were her answer as she flipped the hard-cover book to the beginning and read one more time about the brave fireman, his trusty dog and his bright red fire truck. In just three readings, she had the book memorized and recited the story this time by heart. The boys struggled to stay awake even as sleep claimed them.

First Josh's chin bobbed forward, and then Kale's eyes drifted shut. Ian slumped against her stomach. Sweetness filled her as she set the closed book aside and, still whispering the words, eased the boys back on the mattress. Afraid to move them, she covered them with an afghan she found at the foot of the bed and tiptoed to the door.

The glow of the night-light lit her way and cast enough light for her to take one last look at the trip-lets, identically tousled dark hair and sloping noses, three miniature versions of Matthew lost in dreams.

She eased the door shut and headed down the un-familiar hall, snapping on lights as she went. Twilight had turned to darkness while she'd been getting the boys to bed.

A shadow moved across the open doorway that looked out at the night skies. Before she could even panic, she recognized Dr. Corey's voice coming from the porch. "Matthew, is that you?"

"No, he took Nanna and Patsy home. Patsy wanted to talk to him alone, and I volunteered to stay with the boys."

"Getting pretty close to Matthew, aren't you, from what I hear?"

"We're friends, that's all."

"That's how my wife and I started out, just being friends. The next thing you knew I was proposing to her." His shadowed form filled the threshold. "I know what you and Matthew are up to, trying to marry off Patsy and Nora. I've got eyes, I see what's going on. And believe me, you won't get far. Patsy and I go way back."

"To a falling-out in high school. Helen told us." Hope followed Dr. Corey onto the small front porch. "What happened?"

"Nothing major, and that isn't the reason Patsy won't speak to me, leastwise not these days." He eased down onto the top step. "I owned the plane that crashed and killed her daughter-in-law."

Hope's knees gave out and she took the step beside him. The warm night air carried the scent of juniper from the yard, and she breathed it in, trying to find the right words. "I'm sorry. I had no idea. Matthew could have told me."

"Matthew doesn't hold me responsible and he wouldn't see that his mother would. He's a good man that way, he's got a good heart. Not many men could face the loss of a wife and still find the inner strength to raise three infants with care and love. Not many at all."

"I know he's a good man. The best I've ever met."

"Well, in all your travels, you won't find another to compare, believe me." Emotion rang in the doctor's voice, quiet like a deep river. "My wife died in that plane, too. I was stuck in surgery and they didn't tell me until later. Until it was too late."

"I didn't know. I'm sorry for your loss."

"Me, too." Andrew Corey took a shaky breath. "Grieving is a long journey, slow and painful. But one day, it's over. Not the loss, but the desolation, and you start feeling again. I want Patsy to forgive me, but I don't think she will. Tell me, is that ulcer you had still bothering you?"

Hope didn't comment on the change of subject, surprised that he would remember the few times Nanna had hauled her in to his office over a decade ago. "I wound up in surgery my sophomore year of college. It bothers me now and then, usually whenever I have to deal with my parents."

"Not everyone deserves the parents they get or the children they bear. Families can be tricky things, but luckily they don't need to be permanent. You've grown up and now you can pick your family. And it looks like you're doing a fine job."

Andrew gestured toward the pickup pulling into the paved driveway at the side of the house. She wanted to correct his misimpression, but he was already walking away. Matthew hopped out of the truck, and the two men spoke briefly in low murmurs. Then Dr. Corey waved good-night to her and crossed the driveway to his house.

"How were the boys?" Matthew asked as he paced toward her in the darkness, a shadowed form with shoulders immovably strong. "Did they give you any trouble?"

"Nothing I couldn't handle. You have nice sons. Energetic, but nice." She'd spent many years convincing herself she didn't want children, didn't need them. And yet the tenderness of caring for Matthew's boys lingered in her heart and made her wish. He made her wish. "How did it go with Patsy?"

He hunkered down beside her. "I haven't been in that much trouble with my mother since the night when I was sixteen, took the car without permission and didn't come home until three in the morning."

"You were a bad boy."

"Mom thought I was even worse tonight." He shook his head, tousling his hair. "She told me never to try to marry her off to anyone. Imagine that. I told her I was just following her example."

Remembering Andrew Corey's words, Hope's heart ached. "Maybe she blames him."

"No, she doesn't blame him. She condemns him. I had no idea she was holding this in her heart. It wasn't Andrew's fault. His wife made a pilot error. It might not have happened if he'd been at the stick, but it did. I reminded her that our faith teaches forgiveness, that it isn't her right to hold Andrew accountable. It didn't comfort her."

Matthew looked down at the shadowed ground and didn't tell Hope how helpless he'd felt.

"I'm sorry." Hope's hand, satin-soft, covered his, a connection of affection that made his eyes tear and his heart ache in ways he'd never felt before.

The night brushed her with faint stardust, a silver, shimmering radiance that caressed the high cut of her cheekbones, the delicate shape of her chin and the lush curves of her mouth.

He moved closer to her across the cement steps

until only inches of air separated them. "It seems to me we were interrupted earlier, and I want to correct that."

Her eyes darkened. "You mean when I was helping Josh with the ketchup bottle?"

"Before that." It seemed he couldn't look anywhere but into the depths of her eyes, so dark and luminous. "After I dried your feet with the towel."

"I remember now." She'd remembered all along, her eyes told him that, but she was nervous. And yearning for closeness. And afraid of it.

Just like he was.

"I want you to know that I'm a man who finishes what he starts."

"So, you're going to kiss me?" Her words were tremulous, her lips so close he could sense their movement as she spoke.

"As often as I can." Then not even air separated them, and his mouth slanted over hers. The kiss was like coming home, like comfort and love and contentment all wrapped up in a single, growing emotion filling his heart and spilling over into his soul.

When she withdrew, she was smiling. "Good night, Matthew. I'll see you in church tomorrow."

He watched her breeze down the driveway, a slim shadow against the darkness of the night, her hair blowing in the wind. Holding his heart, she hopped into her Jeep, found her keys and started the engine. He couldn't look away, still unable to breathe, until her vehicle's taillights disappeared in the darkness.

He sat on the step for a long while, lost in thought, forgetting to breathe, watching the stars move across the face of the night. The truth remained as invincible as the stars above.

He loved Hope. With all his heart.

Chapter Thirteen

❧

"It's good to have the house all to myself without a nurse underfoot every time I look." Nanna turned from the counter where her china teapot sat next to an opened package of butter cookies. "Although I will miss you when you go."

"I'll miss you, too." Hope closed the back door and hung her key ring on a row of hooks near the light switch. "It's nearly June. I can't believe time has passed so quickly, and look at you. Another week and you won't need me at all."

"I'll always need my Hope." Nanna held out her arms, and Hope moved into them for a sweet hug. "Tell me all about you and Matthew. Don't look so shocked. I can recognize love when I see it."

"I don't want to be badgered about this tonight. Please." Hope pulled a chair out from the round oak table. "Sit down and stop meddling."

Nanna settled onto the chair's cushion, still frail. Far too frail. "I just thought you might be in need of my advice. Since I've been in your shoes once before."

"Seems to me you're still in those shoes." Hope crossed to the counter where she grabbed the teapot. "Sounds echo in this big old house like loneliness."

"I don't mind so much. I've spent some good years in this house." Nanna smiled. "I have a good many more years to go."

"Yes, you do." Hope set the teapot on the table and the cookies next to it, then spun toward the corner hutch to grab the china cups. "And remember, those years don't need to be spent alone."

The smile faded from Nanna's face. "I know what you're up to and I never should have confided in you. I was like a teenage girl, young again, daydreaming about a man I thought was handsome. But that was all."

"I don't believe you." Hope placed saucers and cups on the muslin cloth, then tapped on the worn leather cover of the closed Bible in the center of the table. "You've been deliberately trying to marry me off to Matthew, proclaiming all the while about the blessings of marriage and the existence of true love. When all this time you're too chicken to take the same advice."

"I give good advice." Nanna's chin shot up. "And I'm not afraid."

"Yes, you are. Helen knows Harold will only see her as a friend. He's made that clear to her, to everyone. Even Helen has told you she thinks you should go for it. She understands. She wants you to be happy."

"She is the oldest friend I have, and if there's any chance that she and Harold will find happiness together, then I will never stand in the way. I could never do that to my friend.''

''Your friend wants that happiness for you.''

'''The greatest love is shown when people lay down their lives for their friends.''' Nanna's lower lip trembled, and she pressed her fingertips to the Bible's cover. '''Love is patient and kind. Love is not jealous or boastful or proud. Love does not demand its own way.'''

'''Seek His will in all you do, and He will direct your paths.''' Hope knelt down beside her grandmother and pressed a kiss to her cheek. ''You are not in control of Harold's heart. And what did you tell me? Life is far too short to forsake God's gifts because we are afraid to accept them.''

''This is what I get, sharing all my wisdom with you.'' Nanna smiled through unshed tears. ''It comes right back at me when I don't need it. Now sit down and tell me. Matthew kissed you, didn't he?''

''I told you, don't go there.'' She felt too confused by what had happened. The claiming brand of his kiss still lingered on her lips, and she needed to be alone to think. ''I'm going to be leaving soon. You know it. I know it. Matthew knows it. Now, read your Bible and let me make my paper roses in peace. The dance is coming up, and Helen needs these so she can decorate the community hall early.''

Hope pulled the box Helen had brought over from the corner, lifted a thin crackling sheet of carnation pink tissue paper from a pile and began scrunching it in one hand.

Nanna shook her head. ''Stubborn people always learn the hard way. You wait and see.''

Later, after putting Nanna to bed and checking the

doors, Hope retreated to her room beneath the eaves.
Restless, that's what she was. The loneliness of the
night called to her, reminding her of the sweetness of
putting the triplets to bed and the precious comfort of
their little bodies tucked against hers. Of the day on
the river. Of racing Matthew on horseback with the
wind on her face and feeling happier than she'd ever
been in her life.

Closing her eyes, shaking her head, she sat down
on the bed. The ancient springs creaked and the old
iron bedstead groaned, and then all was silent. Completely silent.

The memory of Matthew's kiss still touched her
lips, and an ache gathered in her chest, so sweet that
it brought tears to her eyes.

Hadn't she made this mistake before? Memories of
her parents fighting whispered like ghosts in the dark.
Memories of the devastation when Christopher had
shattered her trust. Broken hearts, isn't that where
love led? Even Nanna, with one happy marriage behind her, was afraid. Didn't that show how rare true
love really was? What if she was making a mistake?

Troubled, Hope lifted her Bible from the nightstand
and cradled it. She'd liked Matthew's kiss and she
wanted the excitement and the sweetness of being in
his arms again.

But was it right? The thought terrified her. Love
terrified her. The walls defending her heart were stout
ones, built over time by necessity. How could she
take them down now? Did she trust in Matthew?

The night wind ruffled the curtains at the open window, sending the scent of roses and honeysuckle into
her room. Hope opened her Bible and flipped through
the pages until a verse from Psalms caught her eye.

*Let the morning bring me word of Your unfailing love,
for I have put my trust in You. Show me the way I
should go, for to You I lift up my soul.*

God was holding her heart in His hand. He
wouldn't fail her. Feeling that truth all the way to her
soul, Hope flicked off the light and let the breezes
caress her face. Calm settled over her as she watched
the stars wink and dazzle in a night that felt full of
dreams.

He couldn't get Hope out of his mind. Even though
it was after midnight, Matthew couldn't get to sleep.
He threw back the sheet and paced through the house
in his bare feet, the sound echoing in the infinite darkness.

He ran the water in the tap a long time until it was
cold and he filled a glass. The liquid slid down his
throat cool and refreshing, but it didn't satisfy him.

Nothing would, unless it was another of Hope's
kisses.

Frustrated at himself, he paced to the back door
and turned the knob. The warm breeze didn't help
any, and the shadows only made him feel more alone,
left him remembering the sound of Hope's laughter
in this yard. How the boys had clung to her, laughed
with her, played with her.

She was wrong for them. He knew it. He didn't
have the right to love Hope. They were friends, nothing more. And if his heart felt differently, then that
didn't change the facts. She would be leaving as soon
as Founder's Days were over. Sure, she might not
have said the words, but he knew them to be true.

Nora was nearly well, and after Hope's obligations

were met, she had no reason to stay. Not with the world at her feet and a job that kept her traveling.

"Where's Hope?" Josh's quiet whine cut through the night. "I waked up and she ain't here."

"She had to go home, tiger." Matthew knelt as the boy toddled up to him, sleepy and sweet, and nearly tumbled into his arms.

"I want her to read. I wanna hear my fireman story." Josh rubbed his ear, his whine bordering on a cry.

"Does your ear hurt?"

"Yeah. I want Hope to read." Josh buried his face in Matthew's T-shirt and wept. "I want Hope."

It wasn't until that moment that Matthew realized what he'd done. If he risked his own heart, then he was risking his sons', too.

It wouldn't be an easy visit to make. Matthew drove slower than usual up Nora's driveway and over the whir of the air-conditioning wondered if he had the courage to actually tell Hope what he'd been practicing all morning.

He didn't want to hurt her feelings. He'd never want to do that. Love in his heart burned for her; that was the one thing that hadn't changed. But after three days with a sick boy who didn't understand why Hope couldn't come, Matthew knew he had his answer. There was no other way. He had to ask Hope if she felt what he did, if she loved him and the boys enough to stay before this went any further.

Even if he already knew what her answer would be.

The old farmhouse looked alive with the trees in full leaf and the gardens prospering. Parking in the shade of one of the mature maples, he cut the engine and hopped out into the heat of the day.

"Matthew, is that you?" Hope peered from behind a big flowering bush, a smudge of dirt on her cheek. She was kneeling in the dirt. "I left a message last night and you didn't return it. Is everything okay?"

"Josh has been sick, that's all. Nothing too serious, just a minor earache, and thanks to Dr. Corey he's better now." Matthew stared at the big wicker basket he held. "You and Nora left this at my place."

"Thanks." She stood, brushing dirt from her bare knees as she approached with equally dirty gardening gloves.

It was hard not to remember the feel of her kiss and the sweetness of her in his arms. Hard not to wish for what might never be. He handed her the basket. "Heard from Helen that Nora's getting around well on her cast now."

"This last trip to the doctor showed the bone is nearly mended. Another week, and the cast comes off." Hope set the basket on the nearby bench and wondered why Matthew wouldn't look her in the eye. Was he remembering their kiss? "Helen said we've got the go-ahead to start decorating for the dance. I know it's a busy time of year for you, but maybe you could drop by. We're working tonight."

"I'll see what I can do." A muscle in his jaw jumped, and he stared hard at the ground. "Got a few minutes? I want to talk."

Not about the dance, but the kiss. She knew it. Feeling her face heat, Hope gestured where the garden path led to the back porch. "We can sit in the shade, if you'd like. I'll fetch some iced tea from the kitchen. It's hot today. Summer's definitely here."

"Sounds good."

He didn't sound right—he didn't sound like Matthew. She started to tremble as she led the way across the flagstones and toward the shade at the end of the house. Don't be silly, she scolded herself. Matthew was her friend. Okay, secretly she might, just might, want him to be more.

He clumped up the steps behind her, his work boots heavy on the wood, and cleared his throat. "Hope, I—"

The screen door swung open and Nora held the cordless phone in her free hand. "Matthew, it's about time you showed up to pay attention to my granddaughter. Hope, this is for you. It's your agent. Maybe I'd better tell him to call back...."

"No." Hope grabbed the phone. "Matthew, I'm sorry, but I need to take this. It will only be a minute."

Matthew watched her retreat into the kitchen, already talking. "Her agent, huh?"

"Why, yes," Nora said, with the sparkle back in her voice. "She's got a deadline coming up and whatnot. Her next book is coming out and they want some signing tour or some such. Still, it's important work she does. Have you seen any of her pictures?"

"The ones she took of my boys. They were good."

Pride shimmered in Nora's eyes. "Good? Why, she's better than good. Sit down in that chair, young man, and I'll fetch you an iced tea."

He obeyed, noticing how spry Nora was even in her cast. It was true. She was healing and anyone could see she would be as good as new. And soon.

If he leaned to the left, he could see Hope through the open window. She'd settled into a chair at the far end of the kitchen table and was scribbling something down on a piece of paper.

"Here you go." Nora plunked a glass on the rail beside him and shoved a book into his hands. "Take a look at what my Hope does, photographing light, reminding us of God's brightness."

Matthew had never seen Hope's hardback book of pictures. The cover showed a solar eclipse above an endless sea, both sky and water reflecting all shades of light and darkness. The title and Hope's name flowed in gold print, and beneath, in the corner, was a verse from Job. "Your life will be brighter than the noonday. Any darkness will be as bright as morning."

Inside were powerful images—shafts of light impaling an ancient cathedral's spire, dew droplets on grape vines reflecting the rising sun on a new day, page after page of stunning photographs that made him feel and verses from the Bible that inspired, that gave hope.

"Guess what?" She stood in the doorway, excitement snapping in her eyes. "I just got asked to do a Christmas book."

"This is a good thing." Nora tapped across the porch, arms wide, and wrapped her granddaughter in a hug. "Don't tell me you have to leave now."

"Well, not this minute." Hope turned to him and shook her head. "Matthew, I'm sorry. I've told Nanna not to force my pictures on innocent, unsuspecting people but she does it anyway."

He closed the book and handed it to Hope, but the beautiful images remained, tucked in his heart. "Congratulations on your good news."

"Thanks. Taking pictures on our outings rejuvenated me, I think. I feel ready to start some serious work again.''

"So you're leaving." He could see the excitement shimmering in her eyes, bright and unmistakable.

"Actually, I'm not sure what to do." Hope handed the book to her grandmother and looked vulnerable, far too vulnerable.

He wanted to take her in his arms and protect her, but it wouldn't be right. He had his answer. He'd asked the Lord to guide him, to show him the way.

And this was the answer. Hope would be flying who knew where to take pictures for her books. And he had three little boys to raise.

"Like I said, this is my busy season, and I've got a lot of work piling up." Matthew headed down the steps, heart aching. "I'm going to talk Mom into taking my place on the dance committee."

"I see." She looked crestfallen. "The one she forced you into in the first place?"

"That's right."

"Well, I'll certainly miss you."

Her eyes looked so sad. Was she disappointed in him? "Harold's decided to help me out, but there's still more work than I can do. Plus, I have the boys."

"Sure, I understand." Her chin lifted. "Is there anything I can do for Josh? I could bake more cinnamon rolls."

"No, don't do that." He didn't want to sound harsh, but he was breaking into pieces and he couldn't let her know. "The boys are just fine. Take care, and I really am glad for you."

"Thanks." She looked lost as he stormed away from her, her eyes pinched, her hands loosely clenched at her sides. From her ponytail all the way down to her dirt-streaked sneakers, she looked every inch a country girl, every inch the woman who'd stolen his heart.

But she wasn't. And down deep, he'd known it all along.

Hope thought about Matthew's behavior all through the decorating meeting where about a dozen women sat around tables stacked high with brightly colored tissue roses, making more. Patsy looked awkward when she tried to explain how Matthew truly was busy. The jobs kept coming in and there wasn't enough time in the day.

Hope tried not to read anything into it, but she knew in her heart something had changed between them. It was that kiss, that soul-touching, wondrous kiss that had done it.

He's no fool, she told herself. He has three small boys and more responsibility than she could understand. The last thing he wanted was a romance with a woman who didn't know the first thing about a family, about what made love last.

But that didn't stop her heart from hurting. It was as if the light had gone from her world.

As the evening passed, she felt at home here among old acquaintances renewed. Her best friend from high school showed up and invited her afterward to the café for ice cream sundaes like they used to do when they were schoolgirls.

By the time Hope pulled into the spare stall in Nanna's garage, twilight was advancing, draining the last of the daylight. An owl swept past her when she shut the garage door, and she almost didn't see the green pickup parked in the shadows near the house.

Through the windows open to the fresh breeze, she could see the living room. Nanna looked as if she'd just opened the door for Harold, who was holding something in his hand. Then he moved and she could see he held a potted rosebush.

Accept it, Nanna. Please. Hope watched breathlessly as Nanna hesitated, studying both Harold and his offering, then nodded. Maybe accepting more than just the plant.

Joy filled Hope's heart. Matthew. She had to tell Matthew. She could imagine the twinkle of happiness in his eyes when he heard the news. She could picture how his smile would stretch slowly across his mouth and he would nod, glad for his grandfather-in-law, glad for Nanna.

Then she remembered how Matthew had behaved today and how he'd looked at her. He'd put that distance back in place between them, as he'd done at the beginning. And because of the kiss. The beautiful memory of that tender kiss faded away, tarnished by a growing feeling of failure.

She'd kissed a man who didn't want her, a man who didn't want to be more than friends. Hadn't she known better? Both of them had emphasized over and over again that all they wanted was friendship. She was foolish even to be tempted by a kiss and a dream.

Pain tore at her heart and she stumbled through the darkness, aching for the solitude of the garden, silent and cool this time of night from a late watering. The bench was dry so she sat on it and listened to the night sounds, the harmony of nature, of insects, frogs and owls and the chatter of a nearby raccoon probably playing in the birdbath out back.

She ached to spend one more sun-filled afternoon

with Matthew. She wanted his kisses and to find refuge in his strong arms. She missed the sound of his easy laughter, the jaunty tilt of his half grin and the way he made her feel.

But she should have known. She should have realized that nothing that good could ever happen to her.

Her life alone stretched out before her. If she cried, it was only because she'd touched and lost a dream that had never been hers.

Hope realized why Harold had sounded so eager on the phone when she'd called not twenty minutes ago, and her grip on the steering wheel tightened. Had he turned into a matchmaker, too? Even from a quarter of a mile away on Harold's gravel driveway, she could see Matthew perched on the roof in the hot morning sun.

Okay, I can do this. She guided the Jeep into the shade of the house and tugged a small photo album from beneath the seat, then an envelope and two cardboard portfolios. By the time she'd stepped down from the driver's seat with her arms full, Harold was already halfway down the nearby ladder.

"Howdy, missy. Good to see you this morning. Are those my pictures you got there?" He nimbly hit the ground and started toward her.

"As promised. I can't believe how many pictures I ended up taking of the triplets." She handed him the photo album first.

He flipped through the pages right there, delight on his face, love for his grandsons bright in his eyes. "This is mighty fine work. Mighty fine, indeed. Sure I can't pay you for this?"

"Now how can I charge the man who will be taking my grandmother out on her first date in forty years?" She held out the portfolio and watched as he unfolded the cardboard to reveal three framed blown-up prints, one of each triplet.

"Hope, I don't know what to say."

"Then don't say it. Those are mighty special great grandsons you have."

"Don't I know it. Now, if my plans to court your grandmother work, then that will make you my granddaughter. What do you think about that?"

"I'd be proud to call you my grandfather." Hope's heart ached, and the sound of Matthew's step on the gravel startled her. She hadn't noticed him climb down and now she couldn't look anywhere else. Even if the sight of him reminded her of the terrible mistake she'd almost made by falling in love with him.

His hair was dark with sweat and tousled by the wind. Both the white T-shirt stretched over his broad shoulders and his denim jeans were streaked with dust. "Harold bent my arm and forced me to help him reroof his house. It's good to see you, Hope."

But he didn't look very happy. She noticed the strain tight around his eyes and mouth. "I have some things for you, too. More pictures of the boys for the album I gave you and a set of prints like Harold's."

It was hard, holding back her heart, acting as if she wasn't hurting on the inside. Pride sustained her as she held out the prints and the thick envelope. She hated that her hand trembled.

Matthew stepped close enough to take them, then retreated. "Thanks, Hope. It's mighty good of you."

"It's what I do every day of my life." She didn't know what to say, how to keep from telling him that those prints were a labor of love. If things were different, maybe he might understand, but he was standing a good two yards away, a statement she couldn't miss.

Feeling awkward, hiding her hurt, she took a step toward the Jeep. "I tried to reach Patsy several times before I came out here. I have a set of pictures for her, too."

"Mom took Josh to Dr. Corey this morning for me—saved the baby-sitter a trip."

"Is he still doing better?"

"Sure, just a minor ear infection. He gets them all the time. Andrew was good enough to take a look at him late at night for me, so I made Mom take him back to Andrew, not his son. Should be interesting to hear how it goes."

"Well, let me take these in the house and leave you kids to talk," Harold said. "Hope, if you want to give me Patsy's pictures, I'll make sure she gets them today. Should be going to town anyway later this afternoon, and it'd save you a trip."

"Thanks." Hope leaned across the driver's seat and grabbed the duplicate album and prints. Harold took them from her with a wink, then headed for the house, leaving her alone with Matthew.

"I'm hoping to finish this roof before the heat of the day." He backed toward the ladder, but something flickered in his eyes that she couldn't read. Regret? Sadness?

"I just have one thing to say first." Hope took a deep breath. "I'm sorry about the kiss. It had to have bothered you, but I don't want you upset at me because of it."

"You're sorry." He repeated the words, weighing them. "I am, too. Should we leave it at that?"

"Sure. And I realize that you might not want to take me to the dance, especially since we're no longer on the committee together, so consider yourself free of the obligation."

Matthew nodded, seeing the hurt shadow her eyes and feeling a similar pain in his heart. They'd let it go too far. It was nobody's fault. Knowing Hope, feeling her warmth and sharing her laughter had changed his life for the best. How could he be sorry about that? "Everyone figures you'll be leaving town as soon as Founder's Days are over. Is that true?"

She nodded. "Nanna's getting around so well, she doesn't need me anymore. Her cast comes off Monday morning and so I booked a flight out that afternoon. Since I don't have any other reason to stay." She paused, looking frail and lost somehow. "Do I?"

Did she? This was the chance to ask her how she felt, how she truly felt. To find out if his love was enough to keep her here. He fought the urge to wrap her in his arms, fought every urge to hold her. "You've got pictures to take for your new book. I suppose you need to fly somewhere far away for that."

"Not really. The sun shines even here in Montana." She spoke quietly, leaving much unsaid, and he knew what she was asking.

No, his heart answered. She might stay, but she had the world at her feet. The images from her books lingered in his mind, brilliant, subtle, sublime. She had a calling, and it wasn't here in rural Montana.

On a prayer, he took a deep breath and said the

hardest words he'd ever had to say. "Looks like I'll see you at the dance Friday night."

The silent appeal faded from her luminous eyes. "Yes, I'll see you there."

He watched her turn and hop into her Jeep. Her head was bowed, and she didn't look at him as the warning chime dinged and she shut the door. The photographs he held in his hands felt as heavy as his heart as she fastened her seat belt and started the engine. He couldn't watch her head down the circular lane, driving straight toward the horizon.

His vision was blurry when he went to look at the matted prints—one of each boy, the pictures she took the day they'd drifted down the river with the boys, images captured with a gifted eye and an affectionate heart. Ian's sparkling mischief, Kale's concentrated intelligence, Josh's humble wonder.

If Matthew needed more proof, this was it. He wouldn't be floating the river with Hope through the summers of his life.

Sure, he loved her. He loved her more with each breath he took and with each kindness she showed him and his sons. Even knowing she wasn't right for him didn't stop the love in his heart, or change it, or lessen it, and Matthew felt shattered.

Simply shattered. When Hope left, he would lose his heart again.

Chapter Fourteen

The week had been a tough one for Matthew, dreading the dance to come. He'd tried to get out of it, but Mom hadn't wanted to go alone like some poor middle-aged lady who couldn't find a date, and he'd agreed to be her escort for the night. Oh, he knew what his mom was up to, especially since she wouldn't stop talking about the beautiful pictures Hope had taken of the boys.

The night was warm, the skies clear and the bright lights flooding the street and community hall's parking lot could be seen for blocks. A band was playing bluegrass on a makeshift platform in the far corner of the paved lot, and their snappy harmony lifted spirits and the dancers' feet. Observers ringed the sidelines, drinking from flowered paper cups. The scraps of conversation Matthew heard as he passed included remarks about the current low cattle prices and concern over a possible summer's drought.

Then he saw Hope through the double doors opened to the night breezes. She worked beside one of the McKaslin girls restocking the dessert platters on the cloth-draped tables. Pain filled his heart looking at her. She wore a simple blue dress, understated and elegant like she was, and pearls at her throat. She was busy talking and hadn't noticed him yet.

It hurt to look at her, at this woman who was all of his heart, this woman he couldn't have. Think of the boys, think of her future, and just walk away. He gently guided his mom in the opposite direction. "Let's go look for Nora and Harold. I bet they're dancing."

"Look, there's Hope." Mom tugged him through the door. "Now explain to me again why you've got me on your arm and not that wonderful woman?"

"Can't admit defeat, can you?"

"Not when it comes to my son's welfare." Her hand on his arm squeezed gently, a show of a lifetime's love.

"I'm just as concerned about your welfare." He caught sight of Dr. Corey, only because he'd walked up to the table Hope was restocking. "You wouldn't tell me how it went with Andrew when you took Josh to his office."

"There wasn't much to tell. I was polite."

"I guess that means I can count on you to be polite a second time?" Now it was Matthew's turn to tug his mother gently toward the white-draped tables.

"Matthew, now don't you dare—" Mom started, but Andrew turned around from surveying the refreshments and she stopped protesting, for politeness's sake, apparently. "Hello, Andrew," she said stiffly.

"Patsy." Andrew nodded a welcome. "Matthew. How's young Josh feeling?"

"As good as new. The triplets are with the sitter

tonight.'' Matthew watched Hope behind the table,
her lithe shoulders now stiff, her jaw tight as she
worked. She'd seen him. ''Andrew, would you do me
a favor and dance with my mom? I promised her a
dance, but there's something else I need to do first.''

''Matthew,'' Mom sputtered. ''Andrew, surely you
don't need to—''

''Do this for me,'' Matthew whispered in her ear.
''And forgive the man while you're at it.'' He laid
her hand on Andrew's palm and watched the doctor's
face change, saw the reaction on his mother's.

''My son is far too bossy,'' Patsy commented to
Andrew as he led her through the crowd. ''That's
what happens when they grow taller than you. I
should never have spared the rod with that boy—''

The noise of conversations, the crowd, the music
and the beating of his own heart cut out the rest of
Mom's words. The crowd swallowed them.

''Looks like your mom's had a change of heart.''
Hope didn't look at him across the table as she lifted
a small slice of frosted angel food cake on a doily
from her tray and placed it on one of the serving
platters. ''I hope it works out for the best.''

''I heard about Harold and Nora. Double-dating
with Helen and Claude tonight. That's amazing.''

''If only we could take credit.'' She kept working,
filling the platter with angel food. ''I guess God is
the ultimate matchmaker. We're just mere mortals.''

''We're failures, face it, but at least now maybe
Harold and Nora might find happiness. What my
mom chooses remains to be seen.'' He didn't want to
make small talk with Hope. He didn't want to keep
watching the graceful line of her arm as she worked
refilling the platters, her wrist slim and her move-

ments elegant. Had she come alone? He didn't know, but he bet that when she was done helping out, there would be plenty of men willing and able to dance with her.

If only he could be the one with her tonight. To dance with her. To fold her in his arms and kiss her over and over again beneath God's handiwork of stars and sky. He wanted to hold her, just hold her.

But how he could reach out? What good would come of that?

How could he resist wanting to be with her one last time?

"Would you care to dance?" He heard the words and couldn't believe he'd said them, but he knew in his heart it was what he wanted more than anything else.

"I don't want you to feel obligated." She didn't look at him as she turned and set the empty tray on the pastry cart tucked between the back wall and the tables. The vulnerable sound to her voice made him think that she was hurting, too.

"You know if we aren't seen on that dance floor at least once tonight," he said by way of an excuse, "your grandmother and my mom will be plotting ways to trick us into it."

Her chin sank a notch as she faced him, and the hurt he saw there startled him. "You're right. I know you are. Those women think they're succeeding."

"They're delusional. It's a shame in otherwise sensible women like that." He teased because he couldn't bear to say the words. To admit Nora and his mom had been successful in their matchmaking. He loved Hope with his entire heart.

It didn't hurt so much to admit now. He let some

of the self-doubts slide away, and peace filled his heart.

He led her through the crowd, knowing the entire town was watching as the snappy tune ended abruptly and the sweet chords of a Garth Brooks love song filled the air. Harold climbed down from the platform, slipping his wallet into his back pocket, and winked at him.

"Nanna and Patsy have corrupted Harold." Hope shook her head, but the smallest grin shaped her mouth. "I can't believe what old people are like these days."

"It's a shame. I don't know what this world is coming to." Matthew held out his arms.

He watched her hesitate. Something he couldn't name flickered in her eyes, showed in her heart, and then she stepped forward and he pulled her to his chest.

Holding her was like coming home, like finding respite in a weary world. She was his spring after a hard winter, his dawn after the darkest night. Holding her in his arms made him feel rested and safe, renewed and strong.

Gossamer strands of her silken hair tickled his chin, and he breathed in the spring scent of her and remembered the fields they rode through, dotted with wildflowers. He could hear the faint rhythm of her breathing, feel the beat of her heart, remember the sweet taste of her kiss beneath the midnight sky. How he ached to kiss her again.

If only the song could go on forever, verse and chorus, melody and harmony, lyrics and music, so that he would never have to let her go.

There was a time for everything, and the song

ended. Hope slipped from his arms and he wanted to snatch the moment back, anything to keep her close to him.

But he had the boys, and she had the world. Taking her pictures made her happy, he'd seen it with his own eyes.

"Look." Her touch to his sleeve had him turning.

He hadn't realized another ballad had started, and there was his mother in Andrew Corey's arms with one hand on his shoulder. Saying something low in the doctor's ear, she chuckled as if she didn't have a care in the world.

Matthew had to clear his throat to speak. "I've never seen her look so happy."

"That's something everyone deserves." Hope glanced toward the ring of people and the quiet street beyond. "I need some fresh air. Excuse me."

She took off through the crowd, heels clicking. Too full of longing, too confused, too everything. Her senses spun from being held in his arms, and her heart broke with wanting him. Wanting everything about him. His smile, his humor, his gentleness, his strength.

He was everything she'd ever dreamed of and couldn't have. A family. A real home. His love that threatened to claim every vulnerable place in her heart.

"Hope! Don't run off." His voice echoed eerily on the empty street, nearly drowned out by the loud background noise of the dance. "I just want to make sure you're okay."

"I'm okay."

"You're not *really* okay." He loped easily at her

side, and his fingers curled around her forearm, stopping her.

Steady and strong, his hand. Steady and strong, the man. Her heart made a strange series of bumps as she realized she couldn't escape. Breathless, feeling more vulnerable than she wanted to be, she withdrew from his touch. From the touch she craved. From the closeness she wanted more than anything else in the world.

And what was she going to say to him? Tell him the truth? Tell him that being held by him was a dream she didn't deserve?

"Go back to the dance, Matthew. I can take care of myself." She retreated, walking fast, breaking a little with each step away from him.

He's not going to love you anyway, she told herself, marching down the shadowed street, thankful that he wasn't following her yet. When she looked over her shoulder, he looked ready to, hands fisted, legs braced, the wind tousling his hair.

Their gazes met and locked, and the night stilled. She could only hear the sound of her breathing and the drum of her heart.

He didn't want her. Pain clawed at her heart. Tears blurred her vision and she blinked hard, refusing to let them fall. She kept right on walking down the lonely street, feeling the knot of emotion expand in her chest until she couldn't breathe.

What a fool she'd been. She couldn't deny it any more. She loved him. Loved a man who couldn't love her back. She started walking, stopping only to throw off her heels before heading out of town and into the endless night.

She loved Matthew, with the breadth of her heart and the height of her soul. She wanted to be with him with an intensity she'd never before felt. He was her night and her day, her winter and her spring, and without him, she had nothing.

Choking on a sob, she sank into the tall wild grasses at the side of the road. She let the pain wash over her. Let the storm break inside her heart.

Only God's love lasted. She had that assurance. But what about this love she harbored for Matthew?

She'd forget it, that's what. She'd bury herself in her work and go on. Loneliness didn't hurt as much as love could, as the darkness that came with it.

A darkness she never wanted to know again.

Chapter Fifteen

"**N**ow you're sure about leaving." Nanna crossed the gravel drive at a strong clip, thanks to her new wooden cane. "You can stay here as long as you like. This will always be your home."

"I know, but work's waiting." Hope shut the Jeep's back door, struggling not to give in to the grief heavy in her heart. Leaving was the right thing to do. It was the only thing to do. "Everything's loaded, and I have a plane to catch."

"Give me a call when you head back this way." Nanna lifted her free hand and brushed stray wisps from Hope's face. A gentle touch. A gentle love. "I'm glad they liked those pictures you took while you were here and want more. At least you won't be so far away."

"I'll be close enough to fly in for the weekend now and then." A horrible pain tore through her, blade-sharp, and she blinked back burning tears. She didn't want to leave, to let go of this woman and this magical place. "I'm still going to miss you."

"Now, don't get me started or I'll just cry all afternoon." Nanna held her arms wide, and Hope stepped into them.

"Just keep this in mind, dear one," Nanna whispered in her ear. "'Anything is possible if a person believes.' Let the Lord guide you to the happiness He has in store for you, all right? You're so headstrong and independent, making up your own mind on everything. And always remember that your nanna loves you."

"Not as much as I love you." Hot, painful tears spilled down her cheek, and Hope wished she could hold on forever.

But Nanna moved away, and somehow, Hope managed to climb into the Jeep, find her keys and turn on the engine. Somehow she managed to say goodbye to her grandmother who no longer looked frail or old, but infinitely beautiful standing in the shadow of the giant maples, waving with her free hand.

Hope drove away with more regrets than she could name and more sorrows. She watched the farmhouse become a dot in her rearview mirror and then nothing at all.

This was for the best, she told herself. She had a flight booked for California and home, where she would plan more of her travels. She had deadlines and responsibilities to face, and that's where the Lord was leading her. That's where she was meant to be. She believed that. She had to believe that.

Matthew hadn't asked her to stay, hadn't said he loved her, and even if he did, she'd made up her mind. She was better off alone just like she'd known all along.

Across the golden fields of grasses and up on a

small knoll, she could see Matthew and Harold perched on the McKaslins' sloping roof. She saw them turn in unison to look at her as she sped toward them on the paved road. Loss beat at her heart as she watched Matthew straighten from his work. Even across the span of the field and through the barrier of the windshield, the impact of his gaze felt like a punch to her soul.

She *wouldn't* love him. She refused to let her heart love him. What she felt was a mistake on her part. Chanting that over and over, Hope turned down the McKaslins' driveway and circled around to the rambling ranch house.

At the first sight of Hope's Jeep barreling down the dirt road, Matthew knew she was coming to say goodbye. He kicked himself one more time for not running after her the night of the dance. He'd wanted to comfort her, to find out what was wrong, but fear held him back. Fear that he wasn't enough for her.

"Go on down and say goodbye." Harold didn't look up as he adjusted the new flashing around the chimney. "Maybe this time you can get it right."

Matthew tugged off his work gloves and climbed down the ladder. She was already out of the Jeep and lifting something out of the back by the time he got to her, looking like heaven and the purest of dreams, like the woman who could be the love of his life.

What she didn't look like was a woman who belonged in California. Dressed in jeans and a cotton top, wearing a leather belt and riding boots, her hair long and unbound and dancing in the breeze, she looked like she belonged here in the shadows of the Rocky Mountains where every now and then buffalo still roamed.

He hurt with wanting to hold her close, to kiss her like he had that night when she'd felt a part of him—the best part of him.

Two whole days he'd been praying, searching for a way out of this anguish. Surely God hadn't brought him this far to break his heart all over again. Yet that's sure what it looked like He was doing.

"I got this for the boys. I couldn't resist." Chin up and firm, she held out a colorful box showing a picture of a green lawn and kids in swimsuits running through some kind of child's sprinkler. "I thought they might like it."

"Like it? I'll never get them to stop playing with it." Matthew tried to smile, tried to insert humor into the uneasiness between them and failed. So he took the box. "That was mighty thoughtful of you."

"I really care about your boys." She turned away and shut the back with a snap, but not before he saw her suitcases.

Nothing could be clearer. She was leaving for good. He wanted to stop her. More than he'd ever wanted anything.

The Lord had led him to Hope, led him to Hope's presence and warmth, and for the life of him Matthew couldn't understand why God was letting him hurt like this. Especially after losing Kathy, especially after finding the courage to let go of his grief for her.

Wherever you are leading me, Lord, I go willingly. But show me the way. Show me the way through this. Give me the right words to say.

"I guess this is goodbye." Her words sounded heavy with sorrow. "I've got a flight to catch."

"I know." He choked on the words, wanting to take away her pain and her anguish. Say what's in your heart, a voice within urged him. *Just tell her how you feel.*

But how was he going to do that? How could he find the strength to reach down and speak the truth?

He cleared his throat, wanting to keep her close when he knew he had to set her free. The thing was, she didn't look happy. Her soft oval face looked tight with strain and lined from lack of sleep, and her eyes held shadows dark and deep.

A passage from Isaiah came to him with quiet assurance. *Don't be afraid, for I am with you. I am your God. I will strengthen you. I will help you.*

What did he truly want? Hope. He wanted Hope. To cherish her and treasure her. The world separated them, but could it be possible? What if there was a way to work this out? Did she love him enough to stay and marry him?

The thought terrified him. How could he find the courage to say the words?

He wasn't alone. God was with him. God had led him here.

Strengthened, Matthew took a step closer to the woman he loved with all his heart. "I know you've got a lot of opportunities ahead of you and everyone here figures you'll go far. But if there's ever a way you think you could stay in Montana—"

He stopped short of touching her and gazed into her eyes, into her very soul. "If there's a way you could stay, I want you to know that I love you, deeply and truly. It's as if you complete me, and I've never felt this way before. I want you to marry me. If you think you could settle for a man like me and still be happy."

"Marry you?" Hope couldn't believe what she was

hearing. Had Matthew just proposed? Had he just said he'd loved her? He stood with his hand out, waiting for her touch and she couldn't believe it.

This couldn't be happening. Panic banded around her chest. He'd said the words she longed to hear—words she'd never expected. And there were no more excuses. Not one.

Only the fears in her heart.

A terrible blackness gathered down deep and seemed to fill her. She wanted to run. She needed to escape. Her heart wanted to say yes to the man of her dreams.

What if she failed him and his boys? What if she wasn't enough for him? He was gallant and strong, tender and kind, everything she could never be. Everything she could never deserve.

She could see that now.

"Marry me, Hope." His hands covered hers, and his touch made it clear. He thought she was the most precious love he'd ever known.

The wall protecting her heart crumbled just enough to let in a ray of light. Of hope. She loved him so much. She hadn't realized the power of three simple words. Tears filled her eyes and she tried to find the words. All she had to do was say yes, and he would be hers to love and hold forever. For better or worse.

It was the worse that worried her. The worse, she believed in that. But the better... How did she know if their love would last through the times ahead? It was strong now, but that was no guarantee.

She could fail him. Again, the horrible doubt ripped through her joy, blotting out her one ray of hope. A verse flashed into her mind, one Nanna had recited to her. *Love is patient and kind. Love is not jealous or boastful or proud. Love does not demand its own way.*

She couldn't marry Matthew. Grief clawed like sharp talons across her soul, and she tore her hand away, tears blinding her even though she didn't know she was crying.

"This is because of your job? We could compromise. We could work that out. The boys might like riding in airplanes." So sincere, so steadfast, this tender man who deserved more than she could give him.

True love broke in her heart, deeper, bigger, a new rose budding for the first time, fighting the hard covering that protected it.

"I wouldn't make a good wife," she confessed, battling the tears pressing into her eyes. "I do love you. More than I've loved anyone in my life."

"Whew. I was worried." He smiled, his tender goodness shining through. He was an incredibly good man.

She broke into a million pieces. She spun away, running blindly, finding the Jeep by a miracle, turning her back on a wonderful, perfect dream come true because she couldn't believe in it.

She couldn't risk destroying it.

Anything is possible, a voice inside her urged. But she couldn't trust those words. She couldn't.

To some God gave the gift of singleness, at least that's what she told herself as she drove away.

If anything were possible, then this traffic jam in the middle of the freeway would disappear, Hope thought. But for thirty precious minutes she'd been stuck in a backup a mile from the airport. According to the radio, a wild moose had strolled up an exit ramp onto the freeway, and the game department had to stop traffic to shoo her back into the woods.

While Hope waited, she tried not to think. She didn't want to think about how she'd left Matthew. No, not left him. Ran away from him like a frightened child. Shame filled her. She'd hurt his feelings, hurt him. But what was she going to do? Follow a path that wasn't meant for her? That would end badly for them both? She loved him too much to hurt him and his sons.

Finally they were moving again. Hope raced down the off-ramp and along the service road, palms sweating. She *had* to make this plane. The line was long at the express check-in, and she barely had time to sprint across the terminal, praying the flight was running late.

But there was a line at the security check, and she couldn't find her driver's license, which had fallen out of her wallet and had to be fished out of the depths of her purse. Frustration rose, and she bordered on tears.

Lord, please help me make this plane. Home awaited her—a quiet, one-bedroom condo in a pleasant palm-tree-lined street. A place where she didn't know her neighbors and no one waited for her. There was nothing there but a safe life. The life she wanted God to give her.

Well, that didn't sound right, but it was the truth. The simple unguarded truth.

"Looks like you can catch your flight if you run for it." The security guard smiled at her as he finished inspecting her laptop. "Good luck."

She slid her computer into her carry-on and started

running, but the concourse was crowded and she had to slow down to circle around an impenetrable wall of people.

Father, I could use a little help here. She was doing the right thing, and she could see the coming year unfold before her. Maybe a trip to Italy to finish the photography work she started there, then a long tour of the West. Starting with the Zion National Park in Utah. Yes, that's what she'd do. She'd always been captivated by the vivid beauty of that rugged landscape.

Yes, that's just what would happen. Hope felt the panic like a hard prickly ball in her chest fade into peace. She darted around the last slow-moving person, and the carpeted concourse was clear. And empty.

Please, God, don't let that flight leave. She started running again, her bag banging against her hip, her new boots rubbing at her heels. She passed an empty gate where a flight had already departed. Not hers, but seeing it made her run faster.

She had to get out of here before her heart broke completely.

There it was—the gate agent was taking the boarding pass from the last passenger. The seats were empty, the entire corridor was empty as she sprinted breathlessly toward them.

"Wait! I'm on that flight!"

The agent whipped the ticket and boarding pass from the ticket sleeve with swift efficiency. "They'll hold the door for you. Hurry!"

Hope hitched her strap higher on her shoulder and started running. Her steps pounded like thunder in the narrow passageway, and she could hear the whir of jet engines and the distant sound of a plane taking to the skies.

Nanna's words lingered in her mind. "Anything is possible if a person believes."

She did believe. In God's goodness, in God's grace. But the love with a man was something entirely different. Even one as once-in-a-lifetime as Matthew's love.

We live by faith, not by sight. Remembering the verse made her slow from a run to a walk. *He will not let you stumble and fall; the One who watches over you will not sleep… The Lord stands beside you as your protective shade. The sun will not hurt you by day, nor the moon at night.*

She turned the corner to see a flight attendant holding the door open for her. "Hurry!" she called. "First class is to your left."

Did she keep walking? Or did she trust the Lord with something this frightening? She didn't know. She didn't know what to do.

Then peace filled her heart. She'd spent her entire childhood protecting herself from her family's painful neglect. She'd spent her adult life making sure it didn't happen again. God had been beside her all the way, but she had not trusted Him with this. In everything else—her life, her health, her friends, her travels, her career—but not with the innermost place of her heart.

"Anything is possible if a person believes."

And no matter how it frightened her, she would trust in the Lord. And if He brought Matthew to her, she would find a way to believe. Because the Lord meant good things for her life, and not hurt, not pain.

"I'm sorry," she told the flight attendant.

On shaking knees, Hope took one step back, then another, not knowing what the future held for her—Matthew's rejection or Matthew's love.

Matthew skidded to a halt, his heart breaking at the sight of the passenger jet rolling away from the gate. The sign over the ticket desk confirmed it. Hope's flight to California. A fierce sense of loss, greater than he'd ever known, battered him, and he sank to a nearby bench and put his head in his hands.

She was gone. And it was his own fault. He had no one to blame—not God, not Hope, only himself. He'd lacked the courage to say all the words she needed to hear. The kind of words that didn't come easily to a man who'd lost a wife once before, and in protecting his heart, in keeping back that deepest vulnerability, and he'd lost Hope.

Footsteps tapped toward him, and when he looked up he had to blink to make sure. But it truly was Hope running toward him, tears streaking her face and the carry-on slipping from her hands.

He was on his feet in a flash and his arms were folding her to his chest before he could breathe. In the space of a heartbeat his lips found hers and claimed her with a kiss that reached from the depths of his soul and every last recess of his heart. His entire being sang with the sweet contentment of holding her in his arms, and when she broke the kiss to bury her face in the hollow of his throat, he realized that she was shaking with sobs.

"I couldn't leave." Her tears thickened her voice, already resonant with heartbreak. "But you're here. I can't believe you're here. That you would come for me."

"I will always come for you." He curled his hand around her nape, caressing gently, and yet she shook all the harder.

"You hate me now, don't you? I don't know what to do."

He pressed kisses to her brow, tender with all the love in his heart. "I was afraid all this time. Afraid I could never be enough to hold you here. But God has led me to you, and you are an incredible, impossible gift. I love you, Hope, with all that I am, all that I have, all that I will ever be. And I promise you, my love will never fail you. Never."

Beautiful words. She knew he believed them. She wanted to believe in them, too. But a hard place inside her, the place that had protected her heart all her life, stood fast, like a great unbreachable wall. She couldn't trust. She couldn't believe.

She wanted to. More than anything she'd ever wanted before.

He drew her to his chest again, to the warm shelter of his body, where she could feel his breath in her hair and his heart against her cheek. Where she could feel the anguish fade and the dream begin.

"If you will honor me by being my wife—" he cupped her chin and gently tilted her head back so they were eye to eye, vulnerable one to the other "—then I will promise you this. 'Your life will be brighter than the noonday. Any darkness will be as bright as morning.'"

A terrible rending tore through her, shattering her heart. Aching tears rolled down her cheeks, released from her past, setting her free.

"Now, I'm going to ask you one more time." Love

shone in his eyes, the truest of loves, the greatest of dreams. "Will you complete my life and marry me?"

She was crying too hard to speak. God had led her here, the greatest of matchmakers, the One who knew for certain that their love would last. He'd given her her heart's desire and this man so rare. All she had to do was believe. "Matthew, I'd love to be your wife."

Epilogue

Two months later

"**I** wonder how Harold and Nora's trip to the travel agent is going?" Matthew asked as he shifted the oar in the water, sending the drifting boat safely around the wide river's bend.

Holding Josh's play fishing pole for him, Hope couldn't get enough of looking at her husband. They'd arranged a quick but meaningful ceremony at their church and had spent an impromptu honeymoon in Italy so she could finish up her work there and spend the rest of the summer close to home and the boys.

She caught Ian by the belt before he tipped over the boat. "There's nothing like a Hawaiian honeymoon to start off a marriage."

"Second only to an Italian honeymoon, right?" Mischief twinkled in Matthew's eyes and he grinned, slow and tantalizing. "If my Mom and Andrew keep going the way they're going, then we'll be out of the matchmaking business completely.''

"Sure, as if it wasn't in God's hands all along." Contentment filled her. She had her work, she had her family, and she had Matthew, her love for him growing more with each passing day.

"Careful, Kale," she cautioned. "Don't lean too far over the side. The fish might get a look at you and swim off.''

"But I wanna see 'em!" Kale answered, although he eased back down on his heels.

"Mama, gotta hold me." Josh crawled onto her lap and snuggled against her. "Gonna say the fireman story?"

"Lucky thing for you, I know the whole thing by heart." She set down the pole and ran her free hand lovingly through Josh's tousled hair. Her dulcet voice rose and fell like the breeze with the story's rhythm.

Shade dappled them, mother and sons. Matthew watched, captivated, unable to tear his gaze from the sight of her beauty, of her loving heart. Peace filled him, cool like the river, tranquil like the drowsy afternoon. Hope finished her story and pressed kisses to the boys' heads.

"I love you," she whispered across the length of the boat as the boys snuggled against her.

"I love you more." His heart ached with it, sweetly, so very sweetly. "Forever."

"Forever." Her hand covered his, and his heart soared at her touch. With a quiet prayer, he gave thanks for this beautiful woman he would love for the rest of his days.

* * * * *

Dear Reader,

I was on vacation with my husband, driving through Montana, when I saw an exit sign at the side of the highway. Manhattan, it said, was the next exit. I immediately thought of New York skyscrapers, which seemed completely at odds with the peaceful farmland and majestic mountains surrounding us on all sides. Horses grazed in pastures, and combines could be seen harvesting distant hillsides.

I reached for my notebook. I could feel a story starting, one with the small-town values that I know so well, having grown up in a very small town. I could imagine Matthew, widowed and sad, and a mother who ached at seeing him alone. I could hear Nanna's voice, a woman wanting true happiness for her granddaughter who doesn't believe in love.

This, I knew, would be a story about the ways in which the Lord sends us blessings—rain or shine and without end.

Thank you for choosing *Heaven Sent*.

Best wishes to you,

Jillian Hart

Next month from Steeple Hill's

Love Inspired®

TWIN BLESSINGS
by

Carolyne Aarsen

*Stable, responsible Logan Napier has his hands
full trying to raise his twin ten-year-old nieces by
himself. In desperate need of a tutor for them,
Logan hires unconventional free spirit Sandra
Bachman. Convinced their uncle needs a wife, the
girls try their best to match up Logan and
Sandra. Will these complete opposites discover
they were meant to be together?*

**Don't miss
TWIN BLESSINGS
On sale September 2001**

Love Inspired®